Your Boyfriend Is Hot: Gay Cuckold Erotica
Copyright©2013 Barry Lowe
ISBN 978-1-909934-02-3
Cover art and design by Dawné Dominique

Published by
Lydian Press 2013
Find us on the World Wide Web at
www.lydianpress.com

Your Boyfriend Is Hot

Gay Cuckold Erotica

Barry Lowe

Lydian Press

Contents

Middle Man for Madame Blavatsky was first published in *Middle Men: Gay Erotic Threesomes*, edited by Shane Allison (Cleis Press). All others were first published as individual eBooks by loveyoudivine Alterotica

Introduction:

A Happy Wittol Cuckold

"The allusion to the cuckoo on which the word cuckold is based may not be appreciated by those unfamiliar with the nesting habits of certain varieties of this bird. The female of some Old World cuckoos lays its eggs in the nests of other birds, leaving them to be cared for by the resident nesters. This parasitic tendency has given the female bird a figurative reputation for unfaithfulness as well. Hence in Old French we find the word cucuault, composed of cocu, "cuckoo, cuckold," and the pejorative suffix -ald and used to designate a husband whose wife has wandered afield like the female cuckoo."

http://www.thefreedictionary.com

"What's gay cuckold?" a guy at a party asked me once. "I've heard it mentioned, but I searched everywhere on the net but could find nothing. What I did find was a lot of hetero cuckold movies and written porn. It's everywhere in all its variations and with its own subculture jargon: bulls, breeders, cucks, etc."

I believe one of the reasons he could find numerous examples of straight cuckold erotica is because for heterosexuals, cuckolding is so much more transgressive than it is for gay men because monogamy is not such an indelible priority with a large proportion of our community and because marriage is currently denied most of us. Perhaps when we achieve marriage equality and the corresponding financial and moral burden that accompanies it, gay cuckolding will come into its own.

My facetious answer for a definition of gay cuckolding was, "When one of your friends breaks into your apartment when you're not home and leaves a spinach quiche in your fridge."

Cuckold is one of those old-fashioned words that fell out of favor as a term of moral turpor, originally meaning a male who was married to an unfaithful wife. It has now been rehabilitated by the 'cuck' community to embrace myriad predilections in their subculture. But, basically, if refers to a man who becomes excited at the idea of his wife having sex with another man or group of men. There are so many elements running through this sexual behavior from small-dick humiliation, sub husbands/Dom wives, repressed homosexuality, to the suppressed racist fantasies of men who like to watch their white wives being fucked by black men.

The reasons for it are as various as the behavior. Is the lack of gay cuck erotica and porn because multiple partners is such a part and parcel of ghetto gay activity that you can easily watch your partner at it with strangers? Or is the whole concept of cuckolding alien to gay life? The concept of humiliation and cheating simply doesn't work if the relationship isn't monogamous to begin with, especially when the arching cultural imperative condones slutdom (and I don't use the word slut in a pejorative sense).

For those of a lexicographical bent: a man who knows about his wife fucking around and allows, it is called a wittol.

I remember the first time I got a frisson of excitement over gay cuckolding. It happened while I was watching the movie version of Harvey Fierstein's *Torch Song Trilogy*. There's a scene where his previous lover screws Harvey's current lover unbeknown to the poor cuckold. I got this tingle all through my body and my dick was so hard I almost blew. It had nothing at all to do with my own relationship as my partner and I are not monogamous and I've seen him in action. It doesn't conjure up the same emotions I felt in the movie.

That feeling has rarely happened since, not even on subsequent viewings of the same film, although I enjoy attempting to recapture it by writing stories around the subject.

In this collection of gay cuckold erotica you'll meet men who are complicit in their own 'betrayal' and those to whom it is a wake-up call: from a man at a college reunion who watches as his boyfriend cuckolds him with the bully from his former frat house, a young toy boy whose sexual favors are part of a takeover bid for his lover's company, a callous actor who will hawk his virginal ass to his boyfriend's employer for a chance at the big time, a young man who resorts to tarot in order to experience a threesome, a world famous television chef who enjoys watching his lover put out for fans, and a boyfriend who loves to secretly watch the humiliation of his lover at the hands of his friends and enemies alike.

Your Boyfriend is Hot: Gay Cuckold Erotica includes: *From Here to Fraternity, Stripping His Assets, Indecent Exposure, Middle Man for Madame Blavatsky, A Cook's Tour,* and *Topping the Pizza Delivery Boy (formerly Christmas on the Rocks)* - all previously published as individual eBooks by loveyoudivine Alterotica.

From Here to Fraternity

"Why don't you chow down on this, fag boy?"

I could see temptation in Cory's eyes, probably contemplating his chances of coming out of such a move in one piece. Brick, the football jock, was baiting him by grabbing a handful of his ample crotch through his shorts, encouraged by his two Neanderthal buddies, Scott and Jake.

Is there anything more terrifying than a booze and drug-fueled gang of jocks egging each other on, violence barely suppressed? You learn young to avoid these sorts of situation.

Cory obviously hadn't. He went for the provocative rather than the placatory. "Doesn't look like it's a decent mouthful to me."

That really got Brick off side. If it was one thing Brick was inordinately proud of, it was his dick size. Cory sneered and walked back to chat with other people at the party. Confrontation over. Granted, arch homophobe Brick had been baiting him all night, but it didn't do to retaliate. Unless you were a champ at boxing or something similar.

It had been my skill in the ring that got me accepted by the jock fraternity, Alpha Beta Pi, at college. It was a rare distinction to get into such an exclusive club if you didn't major in football, basketball, and track, with a distinction in hetero gangbang. The frat house was reserved for brainless sporting types who would go on to marry one of the cheer leaders and get a job as a used car salesman before going to fat and dying young of high blood pressure or a heart attack. Brick had achieved the first, was part way to the second, and, much to my regret, had not yet succumbed to the third.

He was a thick shithouse of a man. He'd put on bulk, including a lot of fat. He had the sort of body that drove Cory wild. He was beefy, solid muscle with a beer belly, pecs you could serve a plate on, and biceps that could crack a walnut just by flexing. He was good looking in that dumb jock way they have, and he shaved his head because, as you could tell from the stubble, he was going bald through the center. On him, a shaved head was scorching hot. And he knew it.

He had a sexual appetite to go with it. His wife was continually knocked up which meant he was always on the prowl for new experiences. He was as straight as a ten-inch rule – his purported dick size – and as virulently homophobic as any fundamentalist. Gay boys swooned over him and came away with a split lip, a black eye, or worse. He had a temper on him that was legendary, which is why I feared for Cory.

This whole affair had been a mistake. A disaster waiting to happen. But how can you turn down your hot-as-a-pizza oven blond boyfriend with a body straight out of *Men's Health* when he comes in waving an invitation to your college fraternity's golden anniversary? I'd relegated it to the bin where it should have stayed but where Cory found it. That's why he was waving it in my face excitedly. I wished now that I'd burned the bloody thing.

"This would be so cool, Otis," he was jumping up and down with excitement. "I've never met any of your buddies from college."

There was a good reason for that. Even though I was a bona fide boxing champion, I was one of the un-cool guys albeit I belonged to the top cock frat house. I scraped in on my ability to win medals at boxing, something the brothers had never been good at. They were better than good in a brawl but the 'real' jocks, as they liked to think of themselves, played team sports: football, hockey, basketball, gay bashing. Most of the campus thought they were homophobic assholes, though few had the guts to say it out loud. Except Bobby, and they beat him up for it. Well, to be precise, Brick and his two best mates roughed him up. Just enough that he needed stitches but not enough for the college authorities to become involved. They didn't want to rock the boat. Brick was a top athlete and he brought prestige to the campus. Still did. What with his Used Car lot sponsoring one of the top sporting prizes.

"It's not like it's a school reunion," Cory sulked when I told him there was no way I was going.

"It's even worse than a high school reunion."

It would be all the people I most detested about college life. Sure, I'd been a member of the frat house but most of the time I'd avoided the jocks socially. It'd been a different matter when it came to sporting events. I was expected to attend their games and they, of course, turned out for mine, particularly when it looked as if the frat would finally get its elusive boxing trophy, thus completing a full set of the sports in which it participated.

When Cory doesn't get his own way it's painful, he sulks for days on end. He even went as far as dragging out my old yearbook which had embarrassingly youthful photos of us all sprouting platitudes about the future which most of us would now disown. The photos were taken less than a decade ago but it seemed a lifetime away. Except...

"Who's that?" Cory pointed at Brick. Shane Butler. Football. Frat brother. Nick Name: Brick. Reason: Thick as a...although he thought it was because he was built like a brick shithouse. No one was game enough to contradict him, so the name stuck.

"He's the reason for not revisiting the past," I replied.

Cory looked at me for clarification.

I sighed. "We have history."

Cory was gob smacked. "He's gay?"

"Anything but. Homophobe of the highest order. Fag basher. He and his two buddies permanently scarred a good friend of mine at college. Put him in hospital. Bobby was never the same."

"Shit," Cory muttered in commiseration, although I noticed his cock was still tenting in his trousers. "What did you do?"

"Challenged Brick to a round or two in the ring. Beat the living pulp out of him. He never forgave me. I suspect he never forgot. Threatened he'd get even one day."

"Did he?"

"Not so far. So you can see why I don't want to chance stirring up old wounds."

"You're not scared of him, are you?" Cory was genuinely amused because he knew I had skills in boxing and martial arts and I'd kept myself in great nick. "You could down him before he blinked."

"Nah, not afraid of him like that, but Brick fights dirty."

"Dirty? How?"

"When brute force and superior numbers, namely him and his two goons, don't work he tries to destroy something very precious to the person or persons involved, be it a car, a career…sometimes even a loved one."

"Are you saying that if he couldn't get the better of you physically he'd try get at you through me?"

"Yeah, that's exactly what I'm saying. I've seen him destroy a few marriages in my time."

I could see Cory was fascinated by the concept. I just wanted the subject to go away.

"Just for argument's sake, what would he do to me to get back at you?"

I didn't want to go there. "Well…"

Cory was impatient. "What? He'd do me over physically? Bash the shit out of me?"

"Unlikely. He'd know I'd come gunning for him if he did that."

"What then?"

"Damn it, Cory, what do you think he'd do?" I took deep breaths to calm down. "He'd try to humiliate me publicly by…Put it this way, he knows I put a premium on fidelity."

Cory's eyes opened wide. "You mean he'd try to get me away from you?"

I had to put a stop to this conversation. "To put it crudely, he'd try to fuck you in front of me and all our friends."

Cory snorted. "Not gonna happen. I can take care of myself. You know you're all I'll ever need."

I grunted. I wasn't so sure.

"Sounds like you have a lot of repressed anger inside you, Otis. You need to let it go." He came over and massaged my shoulders. "You're so knotted it's a wonder you don't explode. Here, sit down on the couch and I'll massage that rage away."

If it's one thing I loved about Cory it was his massage skills. I peeled my T-shirt over my head and bared my neck and shoulders to him. He placed a towel against the back of the lounge and warmed a puddle of baby oil in his hands before going to work on my tension. Within half an hour I'd be putty in his hands.

I knew what he was after and it was easier to just go 'mmm' whenever he asked a question or made a suggestion.

"You know this tension is because you haven't addressed the problems of the past?"

"Mmm."

"You need to confront your demons head on. Dispose of them once and for all."

"Mmm."

"Ever since I've known you, you've tied yourself up in knots over your college days. You need to let it out."

"Mmm."

"Here's the perfect opportunity."

"Mmm."

I knew he would go in for the kill any moment now. Then the massage would be over. I'd try to prolong the exquisite feel of his fingers massaging the taut muscles in my shoulders and neck.

"We'll go to the reunion and confront him."

Cory probably expected another "Mmm" but what he got instead was my adamant, "No. We're not going."

To give him credit he didn't begin his sulk straight away. He tried emotional blackmail first.

"Why?"

"I don't want you caught in the crossfire?"

"Meaning?"

"When he can't get to me, he'll take it out on you."

"I can look after myself."

"I know you can. It's just he's more devious than you could possibly know and he'll try to split us up."

"I see." The pout began. "It all boils down to the fact you don't trust me."

"I trust you implicitly," I said. "But he knows what store I put in monogamy and fidelity and he'll use that to cause problems."

"You really think I can't withstand the quite obvious charms of a Neanderthal jock? Give me credit, Otis."

I grabbed his hand and held it tight. "I do, Cory. But Brick's a manipulator. He'll use every nasty trick in the book. For example, you're not known for your ability to withstand alcohol. After a few drinks you get…"

"What?"

"Flirtatious."

"You've never complained before."

"Because I know you're safe with our friends. With Brick you'll be in an alien environment and he'll be one mean son-of-a-bitch."

"That's your trouble, Otis. You always look on the dark side. Why, I bet Brick doesn't even remember you, let alone hold any grudges."

"I really doubt that, Cory."

"For what it's worth, I think you should go. Settle it once and for all."

"It's settled, Cory. We're not going."

Of course, the massage was over, Cory flouncing off to the bathroom to shower the body oil off his hands and arms, leaving me lathered in his displeasure. His parting shot was to call over his shoulder, "I bet you've blown this up out of all proportion. I bet this…Brick… doesn't even remember you, or if he does he's probably forgotten the petty little squabble."

Petty little squabble? If Cory hadn't already slammed the bathroom door, I don't know what I would have done. My blood boiled. I seethed with rage that he could reduce Bobby's week in intensive care with broken ribs, a face that looked like a pink potato, and bruises the color of the sky during a thunderstorm where he'd been kicked while he was down, to the stature of a 'petty squabble.' The physical injuries had been the least of Bobby's problems. Psychologically, he was not the same life-loving gay boy when he came out of hospital. The fun had gone out of his life. Within two months he'd tossed in his studies and gone back to the small town where he grew up and I never heard from him again. Bobby never returned my letters or phone calls. His parents eventually had enough of my barrage of calls, informing me tersely that their son had no wish of further communication with the 'likes of me.'

So ended the greatest relationship of my life. I still missed him. I would never forgive Brick his behavior.

Regardless of my explanation, Cory saw only the good that could come out of scratching off this old scab.

"The only way you can make it better, is to forgive and forget."

It was impossible to do either. Cory was adamant that a meeting between the two of us to thrash out our differences was all it would take. I, however, was not about to change my mind, no matter the sulking, the blackmail, the promise of hot sex. Although I'm adept at a brutal sport and a form of martial arts, I'm a pacifist at heart. I don't seek out conflict: I do my best to avoid it. The easiest way to avoid stirring up the hornet's nest that is Brick Butler was to leave well enough alone.

When Cory didn't get his own way no matter what ruse he attempted, our tense relationship plateaued, almost returning to normal. I say 'almost' because Cory began to spend an inordinate amount of time secreted in the spare bedroom which we both used as an office. He was doing part-time study, working toward a degree in advertising for the years when his career as a top fashion model ceased. His exams were coming up shortly and he was determined to prove as much to himself as to me and his friends that he was more than a pretty face, so he threw himself into his studies enough that his constant bitching about attending the Frat reunion was relegated to obscurity.

Calm descended over the household once Cory realized his residential exams were the same weekend as the dreaded reunion. It had caused a lot of heated debate, both Cory and I hurling insults at each other until we were exhausted and sheepish about what nasty things we'd accused the other of. Cory's complaint that I was unsupportive was unsupported by the evidence but the accusation that I crushed his independence by always taking charge, trivializing his opinions and sidelining his needs had a ring of truth. I was smart enough to keep silent about Cory's so-called 'needs' which usually had more to do with snobbery and affectation than actual legitimate desire. There I go again, squashing his individuality.

I promised to help him as much as I could with his course work but, apart from asking my opinion on the script and storyboard for a television advertisement that was worth a mammoth fifty per cent of his marks, there was little I could do but offer encouragement. He had a weekend in which to shoot, edit and polish his advert before presenting it at the college for final adjudication. I knew he'd shoo it in, and told him so.

Our married life got back to what passed for normal a few days after our disagreement over the reunion although Cory's lovemaking was decidedly lackluster and listless. When I queried him about it he said, "Perhaps I'm not as athletic as usual because I've got a lot on my mind what with exams and stuff."

"What stuff?" I asked as I plunged my cock into his welcoming ass.

"Just job stuff. Nothing important."

He groaned for me but it seemed an act in comparison to his unabated enthusiasm of previous months. If I didn't know better, I would have said that Cory was bored. I even caught him examining his fingernails as I puffed my way to completion.

"Um…Otis?"

"Mmm," I huffed between strokes.

"Has Brick got a big cock?"

I stopped ploughing his ass, totally shocked. "That's a strange thing to ask, especially in the middle of our lovemaking."

"You know how it is," he grinned disarmingly. "The strangest things pop into my head while you're fucking me."

"Well, it sure was a passion killer." I pulled my limp cock out of his ass and he grimaced.

He must have realized the question had been singularly inappropriate. "Sorry, Otis. You know me and my big mouth." In an effort to make it up to me he snuggled against my body so I could spoon him.

I had a hard time controlling my anger and had just about got a lid on it when he tried again. "Well, does he?"

"What does it matter, Cory? You're never likely to see it."

I sat up, indignant that he would ask such a thing.

"I know that," he pouted. "But you know that old saying."

"No, I don't."

"The one about guys with big muscles having small dicks."

"As I was never interested in Brick, I didn't give his cock much more than a glance. I was never likely to go there."

Cory was like a dog with a bone, he simply wouldn't let go. "And?"

"I guess it was bigger than average."

"Thick?"

"Comparatively."

Cory had begun playing with my cock. He got me hard again, pushing me onto my back so he could straddle my cock and ride it like the devil himself, although I knew he was imagining impaling himself on Brick's cock, not mine.

Oh, well, I guess a little fantasy didn't hurt if it spiced up our sex life.

The three weeks up to his exams passed uneventfully with Cory spending more and more time studying, seemingly more moody as the big weekend approached. I had to admit I was looking forward to his absence. It meant three days of lying around doing nothing for the first time since we'd met eighteen months ago. It hadn't registered until now just how high a maintenance lover he was. Not like Bobby…

Damn that invitation. I should have shredded it. Cory's insistent interrogation of my time at college had dredged up memories and feelings I'd long repressed. Brick was the least of them. I hadn't recovered from the distressing rejection by Bobby. It had been five years before; surely it was time I let go. I wondered whether that's why Cory was somewhat bored in his reaction to me: he sensed I still harbored feelings for my former lover.

Bobby and I had mapped out our lives together as if we were both invincible and Brick had slammed full force into our immovable love. At least I thought it was immovable until I came back to our shared apartment one afternoon to find the closet emptied and a scrawled note on the kitchen table, consisting of a single world: Sorry.

The morning of Cory's departure for his exams, we made perfunctory love which was even less satisfying than had I just jerked off. He told me he would be practically uncontactable for most of the time he was away as his movements would be devoted to swatting and exams themselves. He said he'd ring me when he had a spare moment. I wasn't about to hold my breath.

I returned from work to an empty house. Closing the door, I breathed a sigh of relief. It was good to have a little alone time, time I would put to very good use. I stripped out of my constricting work clothes into a pair of shorts and tank top; I had no one to look my best for, ordered a large pizza with everything, and headed for the office to go through our stash of porn DVDs to find something that would be more stimulating than a missing boyfriend.

We kept the DVDs out of sight, not because we were embarrassed but because our home also served as a business center for Cory and occasionally for me as well and we wanted the living area to be as professional as possible. The movies were kept on shelves next to the computer desk and as I searched through the loads of gangbang porn that was Cory's favorite I must have nudged the mouse on the desk for the computer screen flickered to life. It goes into sleep mode after no one has used it for ten minutes.

I was surprised that it still seemed to be logged on. Not only that, it was Cory's email box. He was a stickler for security and he'd never given me his password. His secretiveness annoyed me because I believed lovers should share everything. Perhaps I was naïve to expect that, particularly after such a short period together.

It's not that I wasn't interested in Cory's private emails, but his accusation that I was controlling stung and I thought this might be one of his little traps to test my honesty. I glanced briefly at the subject headings and most of them seemed to be from the university through which he was doing his course. Nothing took my eye immediately so I decided to leave well enough alone. After all, what could he possibly be doing on the computer apart from watching porn, and we both did that.

The pizza was hot and smothered in three cheeses. It was one of my rare indulgences – one that Cory despised because he said it would make me fat. I worked out too hard at the gym for that to happen. Pizza was my once-a-month guilty pleasure. While Cory was away it would be, for once, guilt-free pleasure.

I put the leftovers in the fridge for if there's anything better than steaming hot fresh pizza, it's day-old cold pizza. Somehow the flavors seem to be more intense after a good snooze in the cold. I got myself a beer, an alcoholic beverage that Cory found 'uncouth,' whacked the DVD in the machine, put my feet on the coffee table and settled in for a good old-fashioned wank fest.

I wasn't even to the first money shot on screen when my mobile phone buzzed there was a message. Trust Cory to know when I was up to no good. I retrieved the phone and scrolled through the message. It read simply.

Do you know where your boyfriend is?

As an accompaniment to the message there was a shot of Cory, glass in hand, obviously having a good time. I was pleased he had an opportunity to let his hair down after his weeks of intense study. I just hoped he kept his alcohol intake low and that he left the party soon as he still had exams in the morning.

I texted back a simple, *Enjoy yrself*, and went back to my movie.

The money shot still seemed a long way off although my cock was rock hard and my fist was aching from my constant pumping when my phone buzzed again. I cursed, hoping Cory was not so drunk he was going to keep up a barrage of texts all night.

No written message this time, just a shot of Cory in the midst of a group of partygoers. He'd removed his shirt and was surrounded by a number of men, two of whom were draped casually across his shoulders. They, too, had removed their shirts. I was surprised to see one of them was squeezing Cory's left nipple. He doesn't like them played with because it sends a bolt straight to his cock.

I scrolled back to the sender's number, but it was not one I recognized. The pics weren't from Cory. I was intrigued as to who would be sending them. Maybe a new friend Cory had made at the residential, even though he'd been there only a matter of hours.

Throwing the phone on the lounge next to me, I unpaused the movie and started the slow climb toward orgasm once again by beating my meat. I got to the film's money shot about five minutes later and I'd been edging for almost as long, finally feeling relief a hair's breadth away when the phone buzzed again.

Total atmosphere killer. I grabbed the phone, ready to give my annoying caller a serve by text when I saw more photos. The first was a close-up of Cory with a man's face plastered to his – it was obvious they had their tongues rammed as far down each other's throat as it was possible to get.

The second was a close-up of what was probably Cory's jeans clad ass with a muscular paw squeezing it.

The message said: *Cory is sure having a good time at the frat reunion.*

All thought of porn evaporated. I quickly sent a text message back.

Who r u?

The answer came quickly. It was a pic of four men in various stages of inebriation: Cory, Brick, Scott, and Jake.

Think u can get here b4 we take him down?

I didn't understand: what was Cory doing at the reunion? Why wasn't he…?

I made a dash to the office and brought up Cory's emails. I opened the last email from the university which said they were sorry he had decided to terminate his course as he'd been an exemplary student up until a few weeks ago and they regretted losing him.

Shit!

I scrolled back through his correspondence, my blood turning cold when I came across what I dreaded. There was a receipt for a ticket to the reunion. That wasn't what turned my vitals to ice but rather the email address from whence it originated: it was Brick's email.

There seemed to be a vast correspondence between Brick and Cory for something as simple as a ticket purchase. I opened one at random, then another, and another until I could piece together the story.

Cory seems to have actively pursued Brick, explaining that he wanted to attempt reconciliation between the two of us. Brick had, naturally enough turned down the idea until Cory sent a photo of himself, asking Brick for a recent photo because "I've only seen you as a student in the Yearbook. I'd love to see what you look like today as Otis often comments on your… uh…prowess, if you get my drift."

Brick had obviously been taken with Cory's provocative shot which showed his major asset – his ass – to good effect. In return, Brick had sent a near nude shot that revealed the outline of his prick in his underwear.

Poor stupid naïve Cory had been lured into a trap. He may have had the best of intentions attempting to get Brick and I to reconcile, although his correspondence smacked more of flirtation than rapprochement, but he was playing without knowing what a total bastard Brick is. It did hurt that Cory seemed to be a little too preoccupied with the size, shape and thickness of Brick's cock; although my nemesis kept insisting he was not gay. Maybe not, but if he could wreak revenge he'd stick his cock in anything that was precious to me.

Especially when Cory had revealed we were in a monogamous relationship and that I had strict views on infidelity, threatening that our relationship was over if I ever caught him cheating. Brick led him on, encouraging Cory to admit that our lovemaking lacked excitement, that I didn't totally understand him. And vice versa. Naturally, Brick persuaded him to attend the reunion to chat with my college friends so he could learn more about what made me the person I am today.

I felt betrayed and was tossing up whether to go and rescue my lover or whether to leave him at the mercy of the wolves. If I wanted to salvage our relationship I had better go get him.

I sent off a text, hoping it might give Brick pause in whatever plan he had in mind.

Hands off Cory or u'll answer to me.

The reply was almost instant.

We're just gonna fuck him over a little. Nothing permanent, tho he won't be able to sit down 4 weeks.

I was in my car, flying down the highway on my way out of town. It was fifty miles to the uni but I'd be there in under an hour provided the traffic was good. It was once I cleared the town limits and the traffic lights disappeared. I screamed into the car park outside the frat house, slamming on the brakes in a hail of gravel, burning rubber and black smoke.

I was out of the car and striding toward the sound of revelry when I realized too late...the world went black.

I don't know how long I was out, however, when I came to, I was tied to a chair in what, through my thumping head and blurred vision, appeared to be one of the basement rooms under the frat house. It was sparsely furnished, the walls made of cinder blocks, the floor concrete, a bar squeezed into one corner. Cushions were scattered about the floor and a number of stained mattresses were propped against a wall.

I heard voices.

"Why don't you chow down on this, fag boy?"

"Doesn't look like it's a decent mouthful to me."

I was in and out of consciousness until I groaned and my eyes flew open when my fuzzy brain registered just how much trouble I was in. Cory was staring in my direction, seemingly unperturbed by my predicament. Brick snorted in derision at my groans of pain.

"Your glass jawed boyfriend is no help now, cunt boy!" Brick said, surprising me by the vehemence in his voice and the power in the grip he wrapped around Cory's throat. Brick had obviously been playing it low key up until that point. Now that I was conscious he was breathing hard through his mouth; spit flying out with every word, sliming Cory's face. My treacherous lover didn't look at all perturbed by Brick's outburst. In fact, while Brick still had him in a choke hold, he scraped his fingers across the spit slime on his cheek and licked his fingers clean.

"You're asking for trouble, boy," Brick smiled evilly. "You know what we do to fags around here?"

Cory appeared bored by the question. "I suppose you beat 'em up like all chicken shit jocks when what you should be doing is fuckin' 'em! But you've probably all got small dicks."

"You know I don't have no small dick, fag," Brick roared. With his free hand he unzipped his trousers, lowering them and his briefs until his hard prick sprang free. "Does this look like a fuckin' tiny dick to you?

"From what I can see, a bit above average. Anyway, it's how you use it that's important."

"I never had any complaints," Brick replied.

"Huh, from what I hear your wife is knocked up most of the year. Bet you shove it in and squirt, she gets pregnant, you go and fuck other chicks and do it quick and half-dressed always telling them you gotta hurry before their husband gets home."

I could tell from the startled look on Brick's face that Cory had hit a bull's-eye.

"Bet you've never had a good rough fuck where you can really let yourself go, eh, Brick. How about you Scott? Jake?"

Their silence was all Cory needed.

"You treat chicks like they may break if you fuck 'em too hard. But with fags, you can fuck us as violent as you like and we just beg for it to be even rougher."

I could see Cory's casual attitude to their threats confused them.

The black inky darkness got its fingers into my brain and I lost consciousness again although a nightmare cacophony of sex and raw seduction echoed through my head. Whoever hit me had done a good job of it. I just hoped I didn't have concussion from the battering or the fall onto the asphalt because I didn't know how long my ordeal would last. It proved too painful when I regained my wits to shake the fuzz out of my head. My eyes eventually adjusted after my hearing.

"You like my cock, fag boy?" Brick demanded.

"I love your cock," Cory purred as he took another lick at the shiny spit covered shaft, raising his eyes in adoration of the pile-driving hunk looming above him.

"That's awesome, fag, watching you wrap your pretty lips around my cock. I never had no ho suck as good as you, boy."

Cory doted on praise so those words would spur him on to his best. Before Cory and I hooked up I'd watched him give half-hearted blow jobs and fucks because his partners were stingy on the compliments. Cory only put his heart and soul into it when his fucker was appreciative of his talents.

"You have the best cock I've ever worshipped, Brick." Cory spoke barely above a whisper, which somehow made him sound more erotic, more seductive. "I bet your balls are full of hot jock cum just waiting for me to slurp it down."

He then licked along the underside of Brick's cock until he reached the head, tonguing any oozing pre-cum, making the stud jock tremble.

"You love cock, don't you, fag boy?"

Cory smiled up at my nemesis. "I especially love your cock, Brick." Cory knew how to play the submissive to perfection.

"Then how about you show me how soft that throat of yours is."

Cory positioned himself more comfortably so Brick could hold the back of his head as he guided his long thick cock between Cory's eager lips. They were side on to me and I wondered if Cory had positioned him there deliberately so I could see, suspecting that I might be faking my confused state.

I looked over to Brick's mates who were sprawled out on the filthy couch, snoring fit to wake the dead, their trousers round their ankles, their cocks at half-mast. They looked as if they'd got tired of waiting their turn with my boyfriend.

Brick smiled at me. "You got yourself one nasty cocksucker, Otis. Oh, wait. No, you don't. Not anymore. You don't do cheating. By the time I'm finished with him fucker; his ass will be run ragged. All the frat bros will take turns fucking your toy boy until his asshole gapes like a canyon. He'll be a fuckin' mess, Otis. A cock slut we all use to empty our cock snot into like a whore. See, what he needs is a real man, not a fuckin' queer cunt like you. Too useless to give him what he wants. The slut will do anything for me. Watch."

Brick turned his back to Cory and, bending over, parted his fleshy ass cheeks until his crack was on view.

"Eat my ass, fag. Get your tongue in there."

Cory had always screwed his nose up at the mere idea of rimming whenever I suggested it, but here he was his nose and tongue buried in Brick's fat ass.

"Shit, fag, you got a great tongue. Suck my ass, boy. Eat it."

Cory pushed his face into Brick's hard muscular butt, spreading the cheeks wider to get his tongue in harder.

"Shit, boy, the wife never would do this. Said it was 'dirty.' You don't have no qualms, do you? Fags love to eat jock ass. None of the cheer leaders would go there, not even for the promise of an engagement ring when I was in college. So I had to find fags to help me out. No shortage of them. What I wanted was your buddy's boyfriend chowing down on my ass lips and my cock. Refused me. Told me I was an animal. I showed him. We beat the shit out of him. Taught him a lesson. Rubbed my ass over his face while he lay in the gutter. No one, but no one turns down Brick Butler."

I struggled against the ropes that bound me to the chair, wanting to kill Brick for what he'd done to Bobby.

Cory, conscience tucked away – if he even had one – came up for air, his face covered in saliva and ass funk, before diving back for more.

"Your boyfriend ever eat you out after someone dumps a load up there, eh? Spooge pie. Hey, wouldn't it be great to watch him eat your ass and eat my load. That'd teach the fucker. Hot idea, fag boy?"

Cory mumbled something which Brick took for assent. Brick didn't seem to appreciate the finer points of being rimmed. I guessed he saw it as the ultimate humiliation for the guy doing the rimming and especially humiliating for me to watch my boyfriend eat the ass of my most hated enemy.

"I want to see you swallow a cock while I'm fucking you, fag. Get down on your knees and blow my buddies."

Cory crawled over to the sleeping men and wrapped his lips around Scott's cut weapon, slurping loudly to show Brick he was enjoying the experience. Brick kneeled behind him, aiming his cock at Cory's spread ass. He plunged. It must have hurt. Brick's cock was one of the largest I'd ever seen Cory take on. I noticed a brief grimace because Brick didn't pause long enough to allow Cory to get used to the monster invading his guts.

"This rough enough for you, punk?" Brick pistoned his cock in and out, stretching Cory's elastic sphincter. "I fuck better than that slack assed boyfriend of yours."

Cory raised his mouth off Scott's burgeoning prick. "You fuck better than anyone I ever had, Brick."

Cory had already ceased being my boyfriend in my mind. There was nothing to save of our ill-advised relationship. He was now nothing more than a slab of meat with holes to be filled to overflowing by my frat brothers who would fuck anything if they were drunk enough. Cory's future lay ahead of him like the stained mattresses scattered around the floor and stacked against the wall. He'd be the frat house comfort fag until they couldn't stand the sight of him. His pretty boy looks wouldn't last long under their brutal sexual regime. I'd seen what they did to the girls they lured into their web with the promise of booze, drugs and good times.

I heard a string of expletives from Brick, and Cory begging to be filled with hot spunk. If they thought this was humiliation they were mistaken. I was merely bored, eager to go home and finish jerking off to my favorite DVD. It was much more interesting than the live show in front of me. I wouldn't be going home any time soon. If I knew Brick, and I did, he'd have a lot more nasty things in store for me.

Brick withdrew his cock from Cory ass, then slapped his butt cheeks. "Keep it in there, fag. I want to see you feed my slime to your boyfriend. I want to watch while he eats my cum out of your fucked ass. Climb up on the chair, fag, straddle his face."

I shook my head violently as Cory attempted to find footing on the chair to which I was tied.

"He won't keep still, Brick."

Brick strode over and kicked the chair until I fell backwards, my head banging against the concrete floor.

"Now, just squat over his face. Empty yourself all over him. We'll train him to like it, just like I was gonna train that Bobby cunt he used to hang around with."

Cory stood above me as I writhed in an attempt to free myself, before he squatted, his moist fuckhole already dripping the load Brick had deposited inside him.

"I wouldn't do that if I were you," a voice echoed round the room.

"Who's that?" Brick called, heading for his coat that had been tossed in a heap with his other clothes. He scrounged through the pockets until he produced a lethal looking knife.

Cory hesitated.

My heart beat like it was about to burst. I knew that voice.

"Fag boy, untie Otis." When Cory didn't move fast enough, the voice snapped, "Now!"

Cory kneeled to untie me, his face a knot of concern.

"Leave him," Brick demanded.

The voice continued. "I don't think you're the one in charge any more, Brick. You don't remember me, do you?"

"Show your face and I'll fuckin' carve you into a million pieces."

"Maybe once upon a time that would have scared me, Brick. Not now. It's amazing what five years of therapy can do for a guy. That's why I had to come back tonight to show you the progress I'd made since you…" The voice choked for a moment.

"Don't," I cried out.

"I missed you, Otis. Not a day went by I didn't think about you. You think about me, Otis?"

"Every day."

"Sorry for the dramatics, but I needed time."

"I got the hint. Eventually," I replied.

The look of absolute terror on Brick's face revealed that it had finally dawned on him who was speaking.

"That's right, Brick. It's me. You're invitation came through the mail and I discussed it with my therapist and she thought it was a good idea to visit the past. Lay a few ghosts to rest. Get my revenge. No, that last one is all my own idea, she thinks revenge is unsatisfying. Perhaps, but it will be oh-so-sweet."

Brick manhandled the chair to an upright position so he could hold the knife to my throat, nicking me in the process so that I felt warm blood oozing down under my shirt collar.

"Show yourself, cunt, or I'll stick him. So help me."

"Nothing will help you and your buddies now, Brick."

"This has nothing to do with me," Cory pleaded to the shadows.

"Interesting case. Cory, isn't it? I've been watching you all night, especially after I discovered you were Otis's boyfriend. Where's your taste, Otis?"

"Hey," Cory shouted.

"If I were you, Cory. I'd grab my clothes and make a break for it. Lucky for you I'm not a vindictive man when it comes to strangers. People who have treated me badly are another matter altogether."

Cory grabbed his clothes and ran naked toward the stairs. I called after him, "Cory. Make sure you're out of the house before I get home. Don't even think about taking anything that doesn't belong to you because I'll track you down." Cory disappeared as Bobby emerged from the shadows. He carried a baseball bat which he swung in a menacing fashion.

"It's good to see you again, Bobby," I said. "You look amazing."

He had bulked up, got himself some muscle and a big dose of confidence.

"I like the new you."

"I'm still the old me as far as you're concerned. It's just wrapped in a new shell."

Brick pressed the knife tighter against my throat. "Now ain't this just ducky. A two-fag reunion. All hearts and violins. Come on, Bobby. Why don't we take this up where we left off? You come and suck my ass like a good fag. Either that or your boyfriend here might find himself slipping on a knife."

"If that happens, do you honestly think you'll leave here alive?"

A look of concern flickered across Brick's face and, in that instant of indecision, Bobby crossed the floor and brought the baseball bat down with a sickening thud on Brick's skull. He managed to slice a bigger nick in my throat as he went down.

Bobby smiled but rather than untying me he straddled my lap, leaning over to lick the blood from my neck until the flow almost stopped.

"When did you become a vampire?" I laughed.

"You always tasted good, Otis."

Bobby mashed his mouth against mine and I tasted the coppery blood. I relaxed into the kiss, remembering all the good times we'd spent together. As his tongue explored my mouth I felt Bobby loosening the ropes until my arms were free and I could wrap him in an embrace that showed I was as enamored of him now as I had been five years ago.

For an instant I saw insecurity etched in his face. "Do you think we could…?"

I gave him the only answer I could. I held him as tight as possible, almost crushing the breath out of him, kissing his eyelids as the tears poured from his eyes.

"I never stopped loving you, Bobby. I knew when the time was ripe you'd come back."

There was a moan from the floor before Brick sprang to his feet and ran for freedom. Bobby was too fast for him and slammed the bat into his kidneys. As Brick stood clutching his body in pain, Bobby maneuvered the bat between Brick's legs and…I turned my head away, my testicles crawling into my body in terror. The scream of agony that pierced the air signaled Bobby had hit his mark. I doubled over with sympathy pains although I had no sympathy for Brick.

The cry awoke Brick's henchmen who sized up the situation in an instant and decided retreat was the best option. However, they reckoned without the speed with which Bobby now moved and as they ran for the door they were stopped in their tracks by the swift justice of the bat to their ribs and then to their noses. The sound of splintering bone is not one that I'll soon forget. At least Bobby spared their balls.

The three bullies writhed on the floor as Bobby and I made our way to the exit. "I don't think you boys will want to report this to the police. Simply because Otis and I weren't here. No one saw either of us. Apart from Otis' ex and I'm sure he can be persuaded otherwise. You're lucky I have a forgiving nature, Brick, otherwise that mighty impressive cock of yours would have been skinned to make a cozy for my favorite dildo."

I was still laughing at the outrageous idea as Bobby and I sped the car out of the car park, heading back to the highway, holding hands like old lovers.

Stripping His Assets

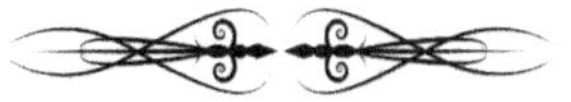

"I'm not saying you're past it, Ted."

But that was exactly what he was saying while pretending a concern for my position that he obviously did not feel. Okay, so I was approaching fifty. Yeah, in gay years that's ancient. Not to me now that my birthday loomed. I didn't feel much different to the young man of twenty-two who'd first started the mail-order business all those years ago. I'd even had the nous to go online before most of my competitors giving me an edge that allowed the company to grow to such an extent that I invited three men to join the board.

One of those men, Sam Weeks, was explaining why he and the others, Doug Boston and Carson Towers, had decided on an 'intervention.' That wasn't their word but that's what it amounted to. And they'd chosen their moment when I was at my most vulnerable.

I was only part listening. They'd come, uninvited, to make me an offer. Too good to refuse, they said. But essentially they wanted me out of my own business so they could run the show. Oh, sure, I'd be titular head, but they were asset strippers and there'd be no company at all to be the tit of in a matter of months, if not weeks. They thought my methods old fashioned, hence the reference to my age, and thought they, being a decade or so younger, were more attuned to the market. Besides, they'd hinted, I had other 'more important' business on my mind.

That business was stretched out on the sun bed below the balcony where we were chatting. That business was called Clay and he was the reason I'd taken my first vacation in twenty years. In an attempt to save my relationship I'd brought him to the cabin for some alone time: he'd been complaining of neglect while I was feeling taken for granted. Our relationship was a scant seven years old and I guess that old cliché about the itch has a grain of truth to it. It didn't help that he was having as much trouble with the hurdle of turning thirty in two years as I was of turning fifty in a month.

Thirty was more important to him because all he had going for him was his looks. Not that they were fading. He was still a magnificent specimen. My wealth meant he could spend his time keeping his body trim, his hair styled, and his butt as bubbly and inviting as a glass of the most expensive champagne.

I cursed myself for letting the others on the board know that I needed time out. The office could easily run for the two weeks I was away. After all, my super-efficient secretary, Casey Scott, knew the day-to-day running of the firm and had my phone number in case of emergencies. I'd have a few words to say to him when I got back.

"Casey is as concerned about your welfare as we are," Doug said when I cursed Casey for revealing my whereabouts.

"If he was so concerned he would have kept his trap shut and left me and Clay in peace."

"I think it's probably a little late in the day to try to save what's left of your relationship," Carson smirked, looking down on Clay's inviting butt.

"That's the pot calling the kettle beige," I snorted.

The three of them were straight and often berated me for allowing Clay to parade around our home in the skimpiest of outfits. Their excuse was that I treated Clay as a commodity in the same sexist way that straight men exhibited trophy wives. They'd know. All three of them explored that route early in their careers. All three were divorced men: Doug was on his third wife, Sam on his second, while Carson was still resolutely single after his acrimonious divorce from his first and only attempt at marriage.

Clay and I had racked up more relationship miles than any of them.

"Besides, Clay does put clothes on when you guys are around, otherwise he'd be totally naked."

"You fags are…"

I had Carson by the throat before he could even finish the sentence.

"You use that word around me or Clay like that and so help me."

Sam intervened, peeling my grip from his fellow board member's neck. I was pleased to see my fingers had left a definite impression. "Come on, Ted. Don't get all defensive. I'm sure Carson didn't mean it that way."

"Oh, I think he did."

Carson was gay friendly on the surface but scratch a little beneath that veneer and he was as homophobic as any redneck. He only put up with Clay because the company made money – lots of it. The company was what provided all of us with the wherewithal for our lives of conspicuous consumption.

"Go on, Carson," Doug hissed. "I think you owe Ted an apology."

Carson made a great display of clearing his throat and mumbling a less-than-sincere 'sorry' amidst the phlegm and the spit before Doug ushered him to the far end of the living room. As they walked away, I heard Doug say, "Don't screw this up, Carson. We've got a lot riding on it."

Sam attempted the 'good cop' role. "He's always been hot headed, Ted. You know his circumstances; cut him a bit of slack."

"His money problems have nothing to do with me," I said. "He's made a very comfortable living out of my company over the years. Very comfortable, indeed. Not my fault if his other investments went ass up in the financial crisis. I warned him those companies were dodgy, the returns too high to be true."

Sam sighed. We'd discussed this on numerous occasions over the past year. While most other companies were going to the wall, I'd managed to steer us through the bad times so we avoided the fiscal cliff, coming out the other end stronger than ever, if you'll let me bastardize my metaphors. "His wife is proving to be a right bitch, threatening him with the courts if he doesn't cough up the sort of money for the kid's maintenance she's used to getting. None of it goes on his son's education. The kid's as thick as two planks."

"Not my concern," I repeated, feeling somewhat churlish that I felt no loyalty to Carson. He'd proven a thorn in my side ever since I'd invited the three of them onto the board when I needed an infusion of cash to expand in the early years. They'd seen the potential and invested enough to allow me to take us to the next level, a competitive player in an overcrowded field.

I kept the company lean and aggressive so that we never had to shed staff like some of our competition when the financial shit hit the fan. The small front office staff had ready access to me so we were quick to adapt to changed circumstances, to develop and implement new ideas – I treated everyone like family. The greatest asset to the company was Casey Scott, a regular whizz when it came to investment. My greatest personal asset was Clay. I know our relationship had begun because he saw me as a sugar daddy. We'd met when he was hired as the male model to front the company's promotion, picking up a lot of gay business through the use of his provocative image. Sure we sexed it up in our ads but a firm butt, a six-pack like a washboard, and a package that promised Nirvana never hurt anyone in the gay market. The early business we'd attracted had remained fairly loyal to us over the years, mainly because we delivered on our promises.

Clay delivered on his as well. I have to admit, I'd been smitten. I asked him to join me after the initial photo shoot and, even though he refutes it, I suspect Clay came along for the ride because he thought his job depended on it. It didn't. He stayed overnight and the sex was comfortable if unimaginative. He stayed for breakfast at which time he got an eyeful of the luxurious surroundings, did a bit of investigation on the net into both me and the company (I know because I found his laptop open at a newspaper article on my net worth), and stayed the weekend. The sex was mightily invigorated on the second night, almost as if he were auditioning. Subsequently he became a lot more attentive to my needs and I grew comfortable with having him around. I don't think either of us expected it to last longer than the summer during which he made himself at home in the coastal cabin where we were now holed up.

He was like the proverbial stray cat that moves in, ingratiates himself, and never leaves. I recall the word 'love' entered the equation some months after our initial meeting and a little later I must have convinced myself that I loved him back. Clay was comfortable and a real ego boost: a man twenty years my junior and hot as fuck. Only his lethargy prevented him from taking up offers of sex outside our relationship. I know he slipped occasionally, especially in the early years because I was insecure and had him trailed by a private detective agency for a number of months.

They'd found remarkably little extra-curricular activity. Clay and I had never broached the subject of fidelity but I eventually decided it was time to make a stand because I'm old-fashioned when it comes to love. The excuse I gave was that I wanted to do away with the necessity for condoms which I found antithetical to good sex. He didn't lie, telling me he'd experimented with a few other men in the early stages of our relationship but found only satisfaction with me. He admitted he preferred being fucked raw and gladly embraced the new regimen after we were tested and given the all-clear.

I had no reason to mistrust him but we both got tested on a regular basis as a precaution. My feelings for him deepened over the years until he became an indispensable part of my life. That's why I was attempting to rekindle if not the flames of our early passion then at least the embers. Clay seemed to think it was worthwhile as well which is why we'd taken this time-out; the one that had been so rudely gate crashed by my three fellow members of the board.

"The company hasn't moved with the times," Sam reiterated. "You've grown a bit stale in the saddle. Your relationship with Clay has suffered as a result."

"Tell me something I don't already know," I replied. "I mean about Clay not the rest of it."

"We think you owe it to yourself and Clay to take time off. Take a real holiday. In all the time I've known you, you've never had more than a week's break here or there and that's usually only been on doctor's orders like after that accident when you broke your arm…"

"The company is my life, Sam," I said, knowing it was a weak excuse.

"We need a new perspective. Young blood. You've been at the helm for so many years—"

I interrupted. "And the company runs like clockwork as a result."

Sam put his hands up in surrender. "All I'm saying is that your mind needs a break so you can return refreshed. Revitalized."

I was wary. "What did you have in mind?"

"Hadn't given it much thought," he shrugged. "Just off the top of my head, how about an around-the-world luxury cruise. How relaxing would that be?"

Boring as bat shit, I thought, but I held my tongue.

Sam went on to extol the virtues of a new mega-cruise ship whose maiden voyage promised untold luxury. He'd already sounded out Clay on the subject and he was 'keen as mustard.' Or so he said. Didn't sound like a spur-of-the-moment idea to me. He already had it all worked out, right down to Clay's involvement. I was somewhat miffed that my boyfriend hadn't the courtesy to inform me of the plot.

"The company will still be here when you get back," Sam said.

In what shape? I wondered.

"I couldn't possibly leave before we discuss the take-over offer by Birmingham's."

"It's a very generous offer," Sam said.

"I suppose Carson's money problems would disappear overnight if we accepted?"

"Look, Ted," Sam moved closer as if he was about to impart some great secret. "You'll find out sooner or later, we're all in a bit of a pickle. The three of us invested in that company you warned us against. The prospect of humungous profit…well, you know how it is."

"Sure do," I said smugly, "The more humungous the projected profit, the more humungous the risk."

"Of course, you were right."

"Now you want me to sell my company just to bail out you three greedy bastards? Your eyes always were too big for your wallets."

"I guess that about sums it up."

"So, why would I sell?"

"At your age, Ted—"

"I'm only eight years older than you."

"And not getting any younger. Think about it, Ted. You're still a comparatively young man. You've got your health. You've got a boyfriend who loves you. Why not spend time with him, enjoy what years you've got left instead of slaving away at the office, stressing over every little thing, getting home so late at night your too exhausted to..."

Sam stopped, his face going red from what he had been about to say.

"Has Clay been complaining to you?"

Sam chose his words carefully. "Not complaining exactly, no." He signaled to Carson and Doug to come and join the conversation. They brought a new bottle of wine with them to top up our glasses. I was glad of a little liquid reinforcement.

I thought attack was the way to go. "So who's Clay been blabbing to about our sex life?"

"Who hasn't he?" Carson sneered.

Doug put a hand on his arm, "That's not helping, Carson."

"He's spoken to the three of you?"

I was gob smacked.

Doug attempted to calm the waters. "It wasn't a complaint really, more of a throwaway comment."

"I see," I said, although I didn't see. "I didn't realize Clay missed my company or my prick so badly."

I'd been deliberately crude because I was annoyed that Clay had discussed our relationship with my fellow shareholders.

"Fuck man, how could you neglect that ass?" Carson slurred drunkenly, leaning over the balustrade to stare at Clay sunbathing on the sun lounge below. Doug shot him a look that I interpreted as telling him to curb his tongue.

I'd always disliked Carson. He was an ugly man; both inside and outside. He was borderline alcohol dependent, had a nasty temper which is why no one put up with him for long, and a mouth like a sewer. I'd had to invite him on board because Doug and Sam refused to part with their cash initially unless Carson was included in the deal. I also knew Carson was an ass man although I'd never known that to extend to the male derrière. No matter, Clay had enough taste to repel the human slug. I made the mistake of saying so.

"It's not like you'll ever get a taste of it."

I saw Sam grip Carson's arm and squeeze until his knuckles turned white. Carson was purple in the face but kept his tongue even though it looked as if he wanted to kill me. I should have known better than to bait him. The situation was fraught with scarcely leashed violence and I wondered how we'd manage to diffuse the situation when help arrived.

A car pulled into the already crowded courtyard, beeping its horn like some young kid squealing in delight at a game he was enjoying; more than could be said for the gritted-teeth tension on the sun deck.

Clay sat up to peer over his sunglasses at the new arrival.

I heard Doug whisper, "Damn, he's early," to Sam.

If I hadn't long before jumped to the conclusion the three of them were up to something, I'd have been hard pressed not to realize it now that Casey had arrived. He climbed out of the car, waving to us on the sun deck, "Pour me whatever it is you're having," he shouted before leaning down for Clay's welcoming peck on the cheek.

I hadn't asked Casey to visit so he must have been reinforcements for the trio who were attempting to persuade me to take a world cruise while they, undoubtedly, stripped the company in my absence and sold it off. Casey would be their big gun in the artillery barrage to come.

An undeclared truce settled over the group although Carson seemed eager to keep up the verbal barrage until he was silenced by Doug. We all seemed to find our wine glasses a source of some import and stared at them as if the solution to the problems of the universe were contained in the white wine we'd been guzzling. I realized I felt light-headed which went some way to explaining my lack of verbal discretion. I'd have to go easy for the remainder of the night if I were to stay one step ahead of this group intervention.

"Hey, guys," Casey smiled as he came out of the living room onto the sun deck.

We all mumbled our greetings then I barged in head first with, "What are you doing here?"

Casey looked startled by the question, glancing between the other three as if to question what was going on. He'd obviously arrived before they could put their scheme into action.

Sam attempted to deflect attention away from Casey by saying, "That wine has made me ravenous. Anyone else hungry?"

Doug picked up on the change of subject. "Yeah, I could go a decent meal. I haven't eaten all day. What about you Carson?"

Instead of agreeing he turned on me, "What do you mean—?"

I was in no mood for a verbal sparring match with Carson. "There's a great steak restaurant in the village." I looked at my watch. "They open early. I can recommend the porterhouse and they have a pretty good wine list for such a small town. It's never likely to feature in the Michelin guide but it's appetizing and quite filling."

I was babbling but only because Carson was mumbling angrily and I needed to stop him before the situation got out of hand. Also, I needed to get my head around what was going on. The fact that Casey had turned up meant I had one less ally.

A general murmur of agreement to eat, then we all headed out to the courtyard, collecting Clay as we passed. I took him his shorts and a casual shirt to cover up his hot body and taut, tight ass. As I had the bigger vehicle, I took Clay, Casey and Sam, while Doug took Carson in his car. I smirked, expecting there would be a few words spoken in heat in the other vehicle. My speculation was confirmed as we passed them on the country dirt road into town and saw them gesticulating wildly at each other.

The food was pleasant and flavorful – what more could you ask? – as was the conversation which never strayed into territory that would make anyone uncomfortable although I sensed Doug had Carson on a tight rein. Carson still looked fit to burst and it had nothing to do with his prodigious appetite.

No one seemed in any hurry to return to the seaside cabin but, eventually, the restaurant wanted to close and we drove back. We'd all imbibed plentifully of the wine but now that the trio were obviously about to get down to the nitty gritty, aided and abetted by Casey, the hard liquor was released from its cabinet. The scotch, brandy and vodka flowed like water. Clay was already three sheets to the wind; he'd never been able to hold his liquor, but then he didn't need to for the forthcoming tête-a-tête. He'd long ago decided all he had to do was lounge around looking cute, preferably in as little clothing as he could get away with. This he did with great aplomb while watching the TV with the sound barely audible in order not to disturb us. His exhibitionism tended to be accentuated by the amount of alcohol he ingested. That night he was quick to discard all his clothing – his excuse was the humidity which made all our clothes cling uncomfortably to our bodies – covering his modesty with a cushion.

He at least was comfortable although I noticed Casey glance over to the lounge from time to time as Clay inadvertently flashed his butt. I couldn't blame him because everyone in the company knew that Clay very definitely sat on his greatest asset and many had tried to sample it for themselves to no avail. Casey had more chance than anyone because he was as young as Clay, and almost as hot. He also had the good sense to be gay. Clay, however, scarcely gave him a look. He probably wasn't wealthy enough.

We men, if you'll excuse the term, adjourned to the sun deck in an effort to get the cooling effects of any recalcitrant breeze that wafted in off the ocean. We sat in silence for a good while sipping at our various drinks, the tension scarcely tethered. Sam was the first to break the silence.

"Have you given any more thought to what I suggested earlier?"

I wasn't going to make it easy for him. "What exactly?"

"The idea of a cruise."

"Is that why Casey's here? As back-up?"

"You know he can run the company while you're away," Doug suggested.

I smiled. "I have every faith in his ability."

Casey had the good graces to look embarrassed by my praise.

"So what's the problem then?" Carson asked aggressively.

Doug patted him on the arm but Carson, emboldened by the liquor he was pouring down his throat, shook him off in irritation.

"Who said there was a problem?"

Carson's face was a dead giveaway. "So you agree to go?"

"The whole idea was dumped on me very unexpectedly just before Casey arrived. I need a little time to hear what Clay thinks about it."

Sam smiled. It reminded me of an alligator ready to pounce on unsuspecting prey. "Why don't we ask him?" He called to Clay who looked up, bleary-eyed, from the program he was watching. "Clay. Come and join us, we have a proposition to put to you."

"Bring some more alcohol with you, we're gonna need it," Carson shouted.

"Is there some reason you guys are so keen to have me out of the way?" I asked without rancor.

"What gives you that idea?" Doug asked in a manner which more than confirmed my opinion.

I shrugged. "Maybe it's the fact you're all going out of you way to get me on this cruise. Maybe it's the fact you all need money and Birmingham's have got that very favorable offer on the table. Or, perhaps it's to do with the fact you've all been taking money out of the company for years and you're about to be found out."

Carson jumped to his feet, knocking over his chair. "How dare you accuse us—"

Doug grimaced. "Sit down, Carson, and for once in your life, be quiet."

Sam tried the reasonable approach. "We've been friends for years, Ted."

"Friendship doesn't give you the green light to siphon off profits illegally."

Three pairs of eyes turned to Casey.

I smiled. "Thank you, gentlemen, for confirming it was Casey who helped cover up the trail. I knew you three were too amateur to manage it on your own, but I never believed my own personal assistant would stoop to such underhand activities. The cover-up was the work of a consummate professional."

"If it wasn't him, then who told you?" Doug asked.

"I've suspected for quite a while that there was something decidedly smelly about the books but I couldn't figure it out. I employed a forensic accountant and it's taken him almost a year to track down the embezzlement…"

"Embezzlement's a very strong word, Ted," Sam warned.

"Okay," I shrugged. "Why don't we call it what it is. Theft."

Carson was all bravado. "So we borrowed a little here and there."

I laughed out loud. "Borrowed? So, you intend paying it back then?"

No one volunteered to return the stolen money.

"As for your use of the word 'little'." I extracted a small notebook from my pocket; flipping through the pages until I found the figures I was after. "As of last September, my informant calculated that over five million dollars has gone missing."

The trio turned their attention to Casey, seeking confirmation. He blanched at the figure but nodded his head.

"Hurry up with those fuckin' drinks," Carson shouted at Clay who'd taken his sweet time. The television program was obviously more interesting than a group of middle-aged men discussing finances.

"What did your last slave die of?" he responded cheekily.

To show his displeasure at being interrupted he stood, allowing the pillow to fall from his crotch so he stood stark naked as he gathered the bottles of spirits and mixers on a tray to bring them out onto the deck, his cock swinging obscenely as he moved around the table. Carson swatted him savagely on the bare butt as he leaned over to place the bottle of liquor and the mixers on the table. "Put some fuckin' clothes on!" Carson then rubbed the tender spot that was already glowing pink against Clay's skin.

"What's the problem?" I asked. "We're all men here and you guys are straight. What? He reminds you of how flabby you three have got sitting behind a desk all day?" I prided myself on the fact my body was still as good as when Clay and I first met.

"I can still turn heads," Sam snapped.

"Besides, you will not tell my partner what to do in my home," I hissed.

Carson guffawed. "Your slut you mean?"

I choked on my drink. "Pardon?"

I saw Clay bristle, glaring at Carson, an eyebrow arched almost in warning.

"Correct me if I'm wrong, but the title for his cabin and land belongs to the company, so it's not yours, it's ours." Carson was trying to get Sam and Doug into the fight which they, so far, had seemed reluctant to join.

"Why don't we stop all this bullshit now," Carson said, dragging a reluctant Clay down onto his lap. "You're not going anywhere, sonny, until we get this sorted out."

Clay struggled half-heartedly but I noticed his cock filled with blood as Carson held him firm.

"We tried doing this the nice way," Sam snarled. "Why the fuck did you have to be so intransigent?"

I was flabbergasted. "It is my company, after all."

Carson sneered. "Not for much longer."

I played my ace. "Might I remind you that I own fifty-one per cent of the shares in this company. My vote will always trump all yours put together."

"If you're so confident, Ted, call a board meeting. Then you'll see the numbers are stacked against you."

"Bullshit!" I snapped.

Doug was all reasonableness. "I think you're overlooking the little fact that Clay there has three per cent of your fifty-one, therefore he's the maker or breaker. I think you'll find Clay's switched allegiances."

"Clay would never betray me. He loves me," I blabbed.

"Loved," Sam said simply. "Past tense."

"You can't ignore a hungry ass like this one and expect it to hang around waiting. So we fed it for you," Carson smirked.

I felt ill at the thought of Carson's cock in my boyfriend's butt.

"We're totally monogamous," I crowed. "Clay would never do that. Not with an ugly cunt like you."

Sam and Doug seemed content now to sit back and let Carson run off at the mouth.

"Reality check," Carson said, then turning to Clay, "Get up on the table, slut. Part those sweet cheeks of yours and let your cuckold boyfriend see where your loyalties lie."

Clay didn't need asking twice. Pushing the bottles and glasses to one side he kneeled on the table pulling his ass cheeks apart with his hands giving me an upfront and personal of his tight, puckered hole.

"Push, slut," Carson commanded.

Clay's asshole quivered and pouted as he strained until eventually a thin film of spunk oozed its way from his hole, dribbling down over his balls.

Sam and Doug had the decency to appear embarrassed.

"Don't go to water now," Carson said triumphantly to his partners. "You guys have fuckin' tagged his ass almost as many times as me. No, don't try to deny it, Doug. I was there that day you fucked poor Clay into the bed. You didn't know I was in the closet watching every minute of your debauchery."

I had to know. "Sam?"

He shrugged. "Even as a straight man, it's very hard not to be tempted by a sweet piece of ass like Clay's."

Casey sounded exasperated. "Am I the only one who hasn't tapped his ass?"

"Looks that way," I replied.

"Easily remedied." Carson spat into Clay's crack, massaging the gob of spit into his sphincter, pushing two fingers into the depths of his ass. "Come on, Casey. Give it a go. You're the only one here who's never had the joy of Clay's second-hand cunt. Go on, baby, fuck him. His ass may have been shagged almost to death but he's still tight enough. Look." Carson plunged three fingers into Clay's hole, slamming him hard before pulling out to show his fingers dripping with stale spooge. "Yeah, Ted, we all gang fucked your little bride this morning while you were packing. Don't think it wasn't fun."

"Now you know where Clay's loyalties lie," Doug said.

Sam couldn't look me in the eye. "I'm sorry, Ted."

Carson was triumphant. "Go on, show your boyfriend what a slut you are. Beg Casey to fuck you. Show him how low you've fallen."

Clay was flushed from all the alcohol he'd consumed and from having Carson's fingers wedged in his frustrated ass. "Come on, Casey, I've wanted that cock of yours in my cum bucket ass since the first day you started at the office. I couldn't have made it more obvious. Fuck me, come on. Don't make me beg. I'll squeeze your cock so tight with my ass cunt lips you'll think you've died and gone to fuck heaven."

Casey seemed mesmerized by Clay's butt. He stood and unzipped, allowing his shorts to fall to the floor. His briefs followed. Kicking them aside he ran his hands lovingly over Clay's smooth ass cheeks.

"I can't say I haven't had a fantasy or two about your hot ass, Clay." His hard cock, already drooling pre-cum, was confirmation of that. "Sorry, boss, but like Clay, I know which side my bread's buttered on. When the winning team throws in a fantasy fuck with the slut of my dreams then that's the cream on the cake."

"Cream in the slut more like it," Carson said taking advantage of Clay's empty mouth by shoving his semi-tumescent cock between my boyfriend's lips as Casey slid into his ass.

I stood up as the two men slammed their cocks and their contempt into my partner. Former partner. It was odd; my heart wasn't broken by his sexual treachery but by the betrayal of my friends, people whom I'd trusted all my life.

I was humbled. "I'll just go and pack."

Carson whooped as his cock choked Clay, forcing snot and mucous out his nose. "We're gonna fuck him just like we're gonna fuck you and your pissant little company."

I walked back inside, Doug already standing to relieve himself of his clothes so he, too, could join in the feast of panthers...

Sam stopped me. "Ted. We got you these."

He handed me an envelope. It contained two tickets for an around-the-world cruise.

"Might help you get over it," he said.

"I doubt it," I replied truthfully.

I took the tickets with me anyway, attempting to block my ears to the grunts of encouragement from Clay as Casey pounded his ass and seared my eardrums with his obscene comments about the utter joy of Clay's snug ass, Sam and Doug impatiently waiting their turn at the latest corporate slut.

By the time I returned, Casey was dressed, having obviously dumped his load. "Can you drive me back?" I enquired.

"I guess I'm all done here?" Casey asked.

Sam nodded.

"I'll see you back in the office on Monday, Sam," Casey said as he picked up my case to carry it to the car. Not every courtesy was dead.

I stumbled behind him, all the fight knocked out of my body.

"Do yourself a favor," Sam called. "Forget about the company, you'll make a nice little profit when we sell to Birmingham's. Take the cruise. Forget about Clay, he's just the company cum dump now."

As I got into Casey's car, I could still see my three former partners fucking Clay into oblivion.

Casey was silent until we were away from the cabin and about five miles down the road.

"Pull into that spot over there," I demanded.

Casey pulled off the road into a clump of trees that hid the vehicle from any passing traffic.

"Come here," I said, pulling him to me, planting my lips on his as I pushed my tongue into his willing mouth, feeling him relax in my embrace.

When we broke for oxygen, he said, "I was so fuckin' tense, Ted. I thought I'd give the whole game away."

I ran my fingers down the side of his face. "No way. You were perfect."

"I didn't think I'd be able to get it up when they wanted me to fuck Clay. Then I imagined I was you and Clay's ass was me and it all fell into place."

"Sorry you had to go through all that, Case."

"Is Clay a better fuck than me?" he enquired.

"Hell, no. Your ass is perfect for my cock and I don't intend to ever let you go."

"You better not," he said as he started the car and pulled out onto the roadway that would take us back to my house that I had already sold at an enormous profit and to the company that Casey and I had gutted financially even as my three partners had skimmed off their measly pittances. There'd be nothing to salvage once Birmingham's sent in the auditors.

"You got the passports and the new IDs?"

"You are now officially Jonathan Piper and I am Blake Pinter. You have a Swiss bank account that should keep you rolling in luxury for the remainder of your life. Plus there's a computer embezzlement trail that leads directly to those four we left back there. They may be out on parole just in time to die."

"Where to, my love?"

"I have in my pocket two first-class tickets to the Bahamas."

"I've always wanted to go there," I said. "Until now I've never had the time."

"Just as well I discovered what those three bastards were up to early on and clued you in otherwise you'd be on that boring boat cruise to nowhere."

I squeezed his knee in appreciation.

Indecent Exposure

The movie was a huge success, unusual for a documentary, even one devoted to the stellar career of the world's greatest living photographer. That would be Lowell Truss. His iconic images adorned the walls of the world's greatest art galleries and museums, as well as the walls of the incredibly rich and unbelievably famous. They also adorned the walls, in poster form, of countless gay boy residences; for Lowell Truss was the most famous purveyor of photographic male erotica the world has ever seen.

Of course, the documentary shattered box office records because it was a warts and all portrayal of the man, the genius, and the unorthodox methods he used to create his incredible works of all-male pulchritude. If photography had been a Renaissance art, Truss would have been the equal of Michelangelo.

I didn't care whether the film was a success or not, or that it had been nominated for so many cultural awards including an Oscar. I could have seen the notorious film when it was first released months back to brouhaha about its graphic images of gay male sexuality, but I'd preferred to wait until my head was in a more tranquil space before I could bring myself to visit that part of my life again. You see, I had…

"Excuse me," the voice called as I hurried across the cinema foyer, eager to sneak away.

I made the mistake of stopping. An attractive young twink, obviously collegiate and nerdy if his clothes and spectacles were anything to go by, bore down on me, his eyes shining with the reverential glow of a fan boy.

"You're Casey McKinney, aren't you? I just saw you in that film about Lowell Truss. You were wonderful," he gushed, then wondering if he'd said the wrong thing because of my lack of warmth, "You *are* wonderful. Much better looking in the flesh."

My lips curled into a semi-smile at the flattery. I knew what the guy wanted. It's what they all wanted when they found out who I am or, rather, who I worked for. They saw me as a stepping stone. After all, I worked for the aforementioned Lowell Truss, a man who had power over men's futures. He could make, sometimes break, a career. When it came to the firmament of male stars, he was God.

If Lowell Truss chose you as a photographic model, you could pick your own career: fashion model, actor, television personality, anything at all that relied on beauty without necessarily having any substance to back it up. All his boys went on to lucrative careers – only their own self-indulgence, be it drugs, alcohol or sexual excess, brought them down.

No one's reputation was tarnished either as a result of modeling for Truss even though it was the worst kept secret that gay sex was the extra ingredient that made his photos the works of art they undoubtedly are. Therefore, I was inured to young models who saw me as a short-cut into Truss's studio and superstardom.

Only one problem: Lowell Truss never used models who were sent to him or recommended by other people. He eschewed the plastic pretty boys that strutted the fashion catwalks of Milan, or who threw their drug fucked bodies about in bars and at rave parties, or whose movie smiles were as false as their straightened teeth. He had an uncanny knack for finding the right men on the street, in cafés, in all walks of life when they were just being themselves. Those men, totally unschooled in the ways of manufactured beauty ruined by the sneer of superiority, were the ones he sought. So, you'll understand why I said coldly to the young man in the cinema foyer, "I can't help you. He chooses his own models. If I were to introduce you, you would stand no chance at all. Besides, it's in my contract that I am forbidden to introduce anyone to him except those people who have to do with his business."

I turned to walk away, hoping that had put an end to the young man's foolishness. I stopped when I heard him laugh, turning to face him when he said, "Look at me. Do I look like the kind of man who has delusions that he could pose for a man who photographs the most beautiful men on the planet?"

He smiled as I gave him the once over, examining him now as I would a fine piece of sirloin at the butcher's. No, a quick scan of his features and what I could ascertain of his body beneath his ill-fitting clothes, he would not make the short-list, even though there was something appealing in his off-kilter plainness. I had seen Lowell's photos transform an ordinary-looking individual into a work of beauty, but I knew this young man was beyond even his Pygmalion powers.

He must have read my agreement in my face because he burst out laughing. "You could have lied," he said. "No one likes to be thought of as ugly."

I assured him, "You're not ugly, by any means."

"Just not a world-class beauty." He didn't seem despondent about that fact.

"So few of us are," I said.

"Can I buy you a coffee?"

I looked at my watch. I had a little time before my pick-up. "Sure, why not?"

We chose an open air café next to the cinema so I could keep an eye open for my lift. I'd explained up front that I might have to leave at a moment's notice but the young man seemed to accept that proviso.

"Damian," he said, holding out his hand.

I shook it, automatically providing my name even though we'd both spent the last two hours watching my supporting antics on the big screen.

We laughed.

"Automatic reflex," I said.

After a waitress took our order, I avoided the inevitable question about Lowell Truss by deflecting attention to the young man.

I hate that question 'What do you do?' because it defines a person by their job, so I've tried various alternatives, none of them particularly suitable. My opening gambit was, "What attracted you to the film, Damian?"

The young man played it cool. "I guess like most out gay men, I have one of Lowell Truss's reproductions in my dorm."

It was no secret that I'm gay; we'd just seen it in graphic close-up for two hours in public.

"I used to stare at it sometimes for ages attempting to decipher what made it so special. Was it the model? Was it the photographer? Was it the lighting? The positioning? Every time I looked, it revealed something new. It had layers – like an onion. I thought if I peeled each layer of artifice away, it would reveal a hollow heart but the more I peeled away the more complex it became. When I heard about the documentary, I thought I'd get some idea on how he did it. But I think I'm as confused as ever."

I sighed. "And you want me to tell you how he did it?"

"No," he said, surprising me. "I think to know would spoil it for me. I want to know about you."

No one ever wanted to know about me; they all wanted the dirt on Lowell Truss. They also wanted my advice on how to attract his attention so they could model for him. To that end, I had a carefully rehearsed spiel that I could regurgitate on demand so my mind could be compiling my shopping list or planning my coming weekend's activities while my mouth did the talking. Even their questions followed a pattern. I was never fully engaged on these occasions.

I didn't know whether to be pleased or disgruntled by the fact Damian had turned expectations on their head and that I would actually have to make an effort when all I'd expected was a chat with an affable young man, filling in time while awaiting my lift.

Thinking about my response, I realized I'd been ambushed. There was no Casey McKinney without Lowell Truss, apart from the mundane that would only interest a prospective lover.

I was young and ambitious, as well as incredibly naïve. I had the hunger, the fire that young people who want to be somebody have burning in the pit of their stomachs. You still possess that sure knowledge that you were really meant to be somebody, before it's beaten out of you through the cynicism of critics and the envious who have their own darlings to promote, and the inexorable grind of having to make a living.

It's okay if you're a prodigy, recognized by some wealthy patron like Robert Mapplethorpe was by Sam Wagstaff, but I was making it on my own without the assistance of prodigy-ness or a sugar daddy. In fact, I had the extra burden of an equally impecunious boyfriend who was attempting to make it as an actor.

Dallas was gorgeous; so good-looking I thought the Fates must have given him to me because they were being such bastards at furthering my career. We were insanely happy as only young people in love can be. We shared the upstairs of a terrace house with an ageing drag queen who made a living MCing at weddings and bar mitzvahs, and her boyfriend who was a long-distance truck driver and obviously a stud of major proportions if the screams of pleasure emanating from their bedroom on his return were anything to go by. They paid half the rent which is more than could be said of the Noah's Ark of vermin and insects that usually crawled in off the street to die in our bathroom or the kitchen.

We didn't notice any of it really; it was just part of everyday living in the inner city. We were happy. I spent my days behind the counter in menswear in a major department store while Dallas rehearsed in theatres the size of postage stamps for stage productions that were so pretentious even the cast and director didn't understand them. I supportively attended with his closest friends and clapped like mad as if we were watching the very best of Broadway. It's what you do. We weren't stupid; we knew that was the way to keep our spirits up because fame and success were just around the next corner. Or the one after.

My artistic outlet was to shoot candid shots of Dallas and his actor buddies as they rehearsed, or solo Dallas looking sexy at home running his lines, or of Willa Catheter in performance at one of the clubs where she worked. Thank God the days of darkrooms and all that messy shit were over because I could not have afforded to indulge my hobby. Cash, for one. Space, for two. Yes, something was lost in the transfer to digital, but many old-timers still did it the old-fashioned way in much the same way that some writers still used a typewriter or wrote in longhand. It's what you're comfortable with, I guess.

I'm a child of the digital age so that's what I used, cropping and improving on my computer. Nothing made me prouder than to attend one of Dallas's performances to see my rehearsal shots taking pride of place in the foyer. Even better was when one appeared in a local newspaper supporting one of the few times a production was reviewed.

But two years on and we were stagnant. Nothing seemed to have changed. It was the same round of casting agents and back-alley performance spaces for Dallas, and the same band of privileged businessmen or predatory queens demanding extra special service from yours truly at the tie counter or in underwear. Until the day of the men's fashion parade.

The store held them twice a year and I did my best to avoid them. They garnered the store a shitload of free publicity but for us salespeople on the floor they were an absolute headache. We had to work at our counters as if a catwalk through the center of the floor was our everyday conditions. That wasn't the worst of it: the models were usually so gorgeous they almost made me renege on my vows to Dallas. Almost. If you think that sounds vain, I have to tell you I was propositioned by at least two or three of the cutest guys every time. I knew it wasn't love and roses and a lifetime commitment, just a quick poke in the men's dunny, but it does wonders for the ego.

This year's parade threatened to be a pinnacle. Not only was it to model the latest male swimwear, the models themselves were the cream of those who had posed for Lowell Truss in the past and as a result had become icons. The man himself would be there.

"Truss himself?" Dallas asked when I complained once more about what a melee it would be.

His interest had perked up when I informed him of the models and I thought I saw him surreptitiously adjust his crotch. It was no big deal, fantasy is not the same as being unfaithful. Dallas had never shown an interest in my place of employment previously but now he began pestering me about the best vantage point to watch the show. It just happened to be at the counter from which I served.

"So if I came along and stood around your counter there's a chance I might run into Lowell Truss?" he asked.

"It's possible," I said. "He has a sleazy reputation, though. And he doesn't choose models who are pushy."

"Are you saying I'm not good enough?"

"Fuck, no. You're cuter than most of the guys he uses. He can make an ordinary guy extraordinary. I wish I knew how he does it."

Dallas wrapped his arms around me. "You don't want to go copying somebody else's style. You want to be your own man."

He only ever did the cuddle move outside the bedroom when he wanted something. "You can come and stand at the counter but I can't under any circumstances get you into the dressing room," I said.

He let me go. "Good enough."

Dallas was a charmer and I thought it would be easy to get himself noticed by the great man. It didn't hurt that on the day in question, Dallas turned up in the huggiest tank top from his wardrobe. It was obviously two sizes too small so it didn't reach the top of his all-too-revealing shorts, so his navel and the bottom of his incredibly defined abs showed, as well as a small tuft of hair that disappeared under his waistband, promising all sorts of excitement if you followed the trail.

"Where is he then?" Dallas whispered.

"He's in the dressing room. He won't appear until the parade begins. Please don't do anything stupid while he's shooting, it's more than my job is worth. He does not like to be interrupted."

"Trust me, Casey. I know what I'm doing."

I doubted it, but I couldn't fault his determination. Nor did I have time to argue because the PA announcement of the parade echoed through the store. This was one of the popular fashion promotions that took place during opening hours in the midst of the selling floors. Its sole purpose was to get people into the building in the hopes they might purchase something, if only a counter lunch in the food hall. The exclusive women's wear parades took place after hours on the same level as the executive offices with minimum disruption to anyone's schedule. Those were for prestige.

We retail staff battened down the hatches and prepared to be swamped. There would be no sales for a good forty-five minutes. We knew to lock the tills and lock the counter displays to damp down pilfering. The noise level would render customer enquiries moot as neither side would be able to hear over the music track to the buff bodies strutting their stuff on the catwalk or over the squeals from excited woman and shrieking queens.

Everything was going well although I noticed Dallas shifting almost imperceptibly toward Lowell Truss who was concentrating all his energy and his talent on the models. They would adorn the spring catalogue, copies of which would disappear as soon as they were released; the pictures used as visual fodder for masturbatory fantasies. Truss's assistant was being crowded by the audience who pushed and shoved to get a better view, the crush threatening to spill out on to the street.

Then it happened. One of the lights atop an unsecured tripod began to wobble, shoved by the mass movement. Dallas was standing nearby and the assistant seemed unaware of any problem. If the lamp fell, it was in danger of crushing a number of patrons if not one of the models or Truss himself. The photographer noticed the illumination on stage flicker and cast an impatient eye toward his assistant for not keeping the light still but he was too intent on the task at hand to notice the peril. He had finished with his first camera and was impatiently clicking his fingers to his assistant to hand him another.

I pushed my way through the crowd in an effort to prevent disaster, collecting more than my fair share of insults and slaps as I shoved people aside. I managed to grab the light stand as it began to topple over, righting it before it clouted the members of the public standing in front of it. Then swiftly I moved it to behind a counter with the minimum of disruption to the parade. Truss glanced over briefly as I repositioned the lamp to give him greater coverage. He dipped his head slightly in acknowledgement.

His assistant had been swallowed up in the crowd and Truss was trying desperately to reach his photographic gear which lay unattended and ripe for theft. Again, I barged through to protect it, shoving people harder than necessary to make them move. This was no time for a simple 'Excuse me.' I grabbed the camera I knew he was after, thrusting it into his impatient fingers while relieving him of the camera he had finished using. A look of surprise flickered across his face but he was a true professional and immediately went back to his task.

For the next half hour or so I matched his every requirement without his asking, including repositioning another light that was nudged off its focus by the crowds. Toward the conclusion of the most successful launch of a swimwear range in the store's history, Truss's assistant had regained control and relieved me so I could go back to my counter. I could not see Dallas anywhere.

The crowd dispersed, the carpenters dismantled the catwalk with ruthless efficiency, the cleaners moved in, Truss's assistant disappeared with the case of cameras and other photographic gear, and Dallas reappeared at the counter.

There was awe in his voice. "That was full on."

"Glad we don't have to put up with that sort of disruption every day."

"Did you see those models? Eh? Most of them weren't even half as hot as I am but the crowd went ape shit over them. Meanwhile, me, ten times better looking and better built, was ignored. See the power of a Lowell Truss photo shoot?"

He didn't require an answer. This was Dallas in his rhetorical 'it's-all-about-me' mood. All he required was a nod of the head and the occasional murmur of agreement to prove you were listening and in agreement with every narcissistic word he uttered. He only stopped his flow of consciousness when he was interrupted by Truss's assistant. I would normally have written 'rudely interrupted' but the assistant came bearing good news.

"Mr. Truss would like to thank you personally for your help during the fashion parade," the assistant said with what I thought was a sneer of dislike.

Dallas had ceased his chatter mid-word at the sound of Truss's name, to listen intently.

"Do thank Mr. Truss for his kindness but I'm unable to leave my counter until my next break which is a good hour away."

"He won't be pleased," the assistant muttered, although I could see he was well pleased with my refusal.

As he turned to walk back with my message which I was sure would be presented with a lot more rudeness than I intended, Dallas said, "Wait. I'll come with you to pass on Casey's message."

I groaned, glaring my disapproval at Dallas's retreating back. I don't think he appreciated that if he fucked up, I could lose my job. Then we'd have no money for those little luxuries of life, such as rent and food. The longer he was gone, the more I worried. Fortunately, a customer interrupted my concern, forcing me to concentrate on his shopping requirements. By the time I had finished, I sensed another waiting patiently for me to serve him.

"May I help…?"

When I looked up, it was Lowell Truss, Dallas beaming beside him. There were people hovering in the background, eager to attract the photographer's attention, not least a number of good-looking young men.

"Oh, Mr. Truss. I'm sorry I kept you waiting."

"On the contrary," he remarked. "It was informative watching you at work. You gave your customer your full attention, I like that. Just as you gave me your full attention when my unfortunate assistant got lost in the maelstrom of humanity. You know your way around cameras, Mr.…" he leaned in to peer at my name tag, "Casey McKinney?"

"I take photos of small theatre productions for their front of house, that sort of thing."

"So you know about lighting?"

"Yes."

"Tell me, do you have a boyfriend?"

I knew Lowell Truss was gay but I didn't expect a proposition like that. I can't have kept the look of surprise from my face because he smiled indulgently. "It's not an offer, Mr. McKinney, merely a prerequisite."

"For what?" I asked.

"Answer the question first."

"Yes, I have a boyfriend," I replied, noticing Dallas was shaking his head urgently. "He's standing beside you."

"Dallas here is your boyfriend?"

"Uh huh."

Dallas looked crestfallen, which made me wonder what he'd been up to.

"Is it a happy relationship?"

I had no hesitation is saying, "Very."

He seemed pleased. He extracted a business card from his wallet and handed it to me. "In that case, please bring me some samples of your best work to this address. Shall we say seven o'clock this evening?"

I readily agreed.

"Be on time," he warned. "And come alone."

I bounced up and down in excitement. I had an invitation from the great Lowell Truss. I couldn't believe my luck. It was a while before I noticed Dallas didn't share my enthusiasm.

"He probably just wants an easy fuck," he said cruelly.

I was pissed off. "Why pick me when he so obviously could have had you?"

My barb obviously hit a raw nerve because Dallas stormed off. What had gone on in the dressing room for the swimwear parade? What offers had been made?

I stewed over those questions all morning until I forgot them in the day-to-day business of retailing. I was reminded of them again when I got home to a barrage of insecurity from Dallas who kept insisting I recommit to our vows of fidelity. He was so insistent I almost lost my temper with him, something I rarely do even when he is a constant aggravation.

"Look," I said angrily. "I don't know what promises you made to him in the dressing room but you seemed mighty keen that I not reveal our relationship." He looked stricken by my accusation. "But I don't have any intention of having sex with the ugly old cunt." It was not a word I used often but I felt my denial needed it for added emphasis.

Lowell Truss himself was not a thing of beauty, regardless of the work he produced. I suppose there's a dissertation waiting to be written on the correlation between the man's rather plain features – that's putting it kindly – and his exquisite photography. I didn't look on him as a prospective sex partner, not even in exchange for help furthering my career in the business. Granted, I was curious as to why he wanted to see me and my work, but that would be answered soon enough. Right now, the last thing I needed was a clingy boyfriend working out his residual guilt by projecting it onto my predicted behavior.

After I'd snapped at his accusations, I reiterated my love and the fact I had no intention of breaking my vows of fidelity, which seemed to satisfy him for the moment. He saved his interference for when I was choosing what I considered my best work which, to his chagrin, didn't always include him.

I was exasperated. "If you're in every photograph I show him, don't you think that's just a little obvious?"

He didn't. I pretended to accept his input, noting mentally to put his shots at the bottom of the portfolio. That his choices had more to do with his impressing Lowell Truss as a model than highlighting my skills as a photographer became apparent when Dallas eventually pulled out half a dozen photos from our private stash. These were the raunchy private shots revealing him in all his rampant glory and were never meant to be seen by anyone but us. I felt sick in the stomach that he would so openly invite Truss's attention. My photographs were crude and pornographic where Truss's were subtle and erotic.

There was no point arguing with Dallas and I mutely added his photographs to the pile. As I showered for the big meeting, he forced his way into the bathroom and fucked me hard under the spray as if marking me as his territory, reminding me to whom my body, if not my heart, belonged. There was nothing romantic about the sex, just rough animal passion that spoke volumes about his insecurities. He demanded I answer 'Who's your master, eh?' when he grabbed my hair, pulling my face into the stream of hot water so I felt like I was drowning. I answered as best I could because I did love the bastard although I began to wonder where our relationship would stand once his career took off.

I felt disloyal when I left most of the pictures of Dallas in the car.

Truss welcomed me with a warmth that made me wary although he made no unexpected lunges or improper suggestions. In fact, he was charming. Once he'd ascertained my bona fides as an amateur photographer, he showed me the originals of some of his best known works allowing me my own observations which he called 'astute without pandering,' then took me into the elaborate studio, attached to his house. It was my dream set-up and I could have spent hours there just examining his cameras and the lighting.

His assistant was setting up for the next day's shoot and was not pleased to see me. Truss had already been through my portfolio, generous in his praise of my ability while critical of some aspects of what I had created. It would have been easy to make excuses about lack of time or cash or proper equipment but I was being mentored, if only for an evening, by the greatest photographer of the era, so it paid to listen. Once I got over the reluctance to hear criticism I realized I was getting a Master Class in my field of endeavor and, as such, there was no price too high to pay.

Truss treated me as, if not quite an equal, at least as if he took my work seriously.

When he handed me one of his expensive cameras and told his assistant to model for me, I felt blessed. I didn't attempt to reproduce Truss's own style but instead went with my strengths, occasionally readjusting the lights, moving the assistant as I would a prop, until I had what I thought were a good dozen or so shots. Truss watched without comment. When I had finished, I made sure I thanked the surly assistant and readjusted the lights to the position they had been in before I began.

Back in the house proper, Truss allowed me access to his computer where he asked me to choose what I considered the best shots I'd taken and to bring them into the dining room in about half an hour when the meal would be served. Fortunately, I had used the software Truss favored and was able to crop and perfect my hurried work in time to present the images which pleased me most by the time the food was on the table.

We talked generalities as we ate, Truss particularly interested in my relationship with Dallas. He asked about its longevity, whether I thought it would last, before getting into more specifically personal territory.

"It's definitely a love match then?" he asked.

I answered without hesitation. "Definitely."

That seemed to please him.

I'd been drinking steadily to calm my nerves throughout the meal and I was feeling very light-headed, my tongue loosened more than was comfortable.

"Why are you so interested in my relationship?" I asked. "Do you have intentions of seducing me later?"

"If I did?"

"Then I would have to refuse."

He seemed more amused than distressed by my rebuff. Perhaps I'd misread the signs.

"What if I offered you a job as my assistant?"

"That would be something I had never dreamed would be within the realms of possibility," I replied, cursing myself that I was such a moral coward. "But I would still refuse."

My answer delighted him.

"No problems at home in the sex department?" he asked innocently.

His question took me so much by surprise, plus I was having such a wonderful time, that I blurted out the one splinter in my relationship with Dallas. "I do get tired of his selfish attitude sometimes."

"Oh?"

"He tops exclusively. Okay, I'm basically passive. I love being on the receiving end, but I would like a little variety every now and then."

"Have you thought of scratching that itch elsewhere?"

"Never."

"Good. I never use the assistance of anyone who is not in a stable relationship."

He looked over the photographs I had taken of his assistant, complimenting me on the composition, the lighting, and all the things I felt were my strong suits, picking out a number of spots where I could improve. I agreed with all but one, and boldly explained that one area which he thought of as a blemish I thought of as what made my work distinctive.

He shrugged. "Perhaps." There was a long pause. "What are you doing tomorrow?"

"I'm working," I replied.

"Can you take the day off?"

"I could call in sick, I suppose, if the reason were good enough."

"What if I asked you to assist on my studio shoot tomorrow? Would that be reason enough?"

"Shit, yeah."

My enthusiasm was tempered with the niggling idea that Truss would make his sexual advances more obvious at that time, thus the reason for enquiring so closely about my sexual preferences and my relationship.

I had no loyalty to the company, especially given the way they'd treated me after the swimwear parade was over. I'd been reported as missing from my counter and although I had various witnesses to my gallant effort to save the store being sued if the lighting stand had fallen on some poor customer or one of the models, thus saving them millions, they saw fit to dock my salary a quarter day's pay for my infringement of my working conditions.

Truss stood up from the table, offered me his hand, dismissing me with, "Be here at ten o'clock, dress casual, come alone."

He showed me to the door.

Damian had not interrupted my story. I'd had to check from time to time to ensure I hadn't put him to sleep.

"You should write an autobiography," he said. "That was fascinating. What was the next day like?"

I knew his questioning would eventually get back to the subject of Truss but I had an out because my lift arrived in the nick of time. The driver beeped his horn to attract my attention.

"You'll have to excuse me, my lift has arrived."

I called for the check but when the waiter brought it, Damian reached for it first. "It's the least I can do. Thank you for a wonderful conclusion to the day. I hope we meet again some time."

I shook his hand. As he walked into the café to pay, I headed to the friend who was picking me up. I got into the car, hugging Stefan, kissing him on the cheek.

"Who's the young man?" he asked.

"Someone who was at the film and recognized me."

"Cute."

"Another Lowell Truss groupie, although he listened to the story of my life with what seemed genuine interest."

Stefan sighed. "You know you're an interesting man in your own right, Casey. I just wish you could see it."

"Perhaps you're right." But I didn't believe it.

Stefan didn't take off right away which was unusual as he was parked in a No Standing zone. I understood why when Damian emerged from the café and seeing me still there, waved his goodbye. Stefan beeped, signaling him to come over. He powered down the window so that when Damian leaned in, Stefan said, "Can we give you a lift?"

"That would be wonderful," he smiled. "I was just wondering how I was going to get home."

"Hop in," Stefan said.

Damian and Stefan got on so well together I wondered whether Stefan fancied him, especially when he suggested, "I have an idea. Why don't you join us for dinner? I'm taking Casey to that smart new trattoria everyone is raving about…"

I was half-turned in my seat so I saw Damian's hand go to his wallet. Stefan must have seen the same thing in his rear vision mirror.

"It's on me," Stefan said. "I'm asking so I'm paying."

There was a flicker of uncertainty before Damian gave in. "I'd love to, as long as it's no bother."

"No bother at all," Stefan said, nudging me with his foot.

On the drive we learned Damian was at university studying art. He was currently at that point where the lectures concerned the history of photographic art which is another reason he was at the film. He was, also, like most students without an economically supportive family, just keeping his nose above the breadline.

At the popular Italian restaurant my celebrity gained us a table in the rear, I eschew the spotlight, and Damian began the questions again.

"What happened when you got home after the meal with Truss?" he asked

Dallas was waiting for me when I got home. My semi-inebriated state didn't please him but he still kissed me warmly, ramming his tongue into my mouth, running it along my teeth sucking my tongue into his mouth. He led me into the bedroom where he undressed me and pushed me onto the bed naked. He didn't bother removing his clothes although he was running his fingers along my ass crack. He leaned over to slip my cock in his mouth, something he rarely does, but it was more akin to tasting it rather than sucking. When his fingers disappeared into my ass and he rooted around as if searching, I knew what his game was.

I pushed him off. "No, I did not suck him off. No, he did not suck my cock. No, I did not fuck him. And, no, he did not fuck me. We both remained fully clothed, there was no sexual activity, there never will be."

I said it as sarcastically as possible, but it must have escaped Dallas for he smiled.

"Nice to see you trust me," I sneered.

"You must admit you came home a little the worse for wear. What was I supposed to think?"

I left that accusation alone. Surely, when I gave him the good news, he'd be pleased.

He wasn't. "What does the old bastard want?"

"He doesn't want anything, Dallas. But it's a great opportunity for me to learn."

"What about your job? We can't afford for you to lose that."

"I'll call in sick. I have enough days up my sleeve so I won't lose anything. Except that miserable quarter-day they docked me."

"I guess it's all right if you go."

I wasn't asking his permission, but I bit my tongue.

"Maybe I can come with you."

"He said to come alone."

"You can see why I worry," Dallas huffed.

This could so easily have turned into an argument. Why he'd be more concerned about my day with a genuine genius when he spent all his days working with sleazy directors and producers, notorious for their use of the casting couch, I couldn't tell. I'd never queried his fidelity, I didn't know why he was so concerned about mine. I had never given him any reason to worry.

"What did he think of my shots?" Dallas asked, finally getting to the crux of the matter.

Choosing my words carefully, I replied, "He spoke mainly about my photographs, their composition and lighting, the techniques I used. It wasn't about the models. However, he did say that you were a, let me get his words exactly, 'a striking young man whose good looks and superb physique will open many doors' for you in future. He thinks you will be a major talent."

"So, he wants to use me as a model then?"

"From what I've read he likes to discover his own models. Anyone recommended to him is automatically disqualified."

"But you could still put in a good word for me, couldn't you? You know, just in passing."

"Of course, I will." I had no intention of doing so, and turned over so Dallas couldn't see the lie in my eyes.

The next morning, I awoke enthusiastic and headache-free, Dallas more attentive than usual. I felt guilty that I wasn't going to harass Truss about my boyfriend. This was my opportunity, not his. I was back at the house on the dot of ten.

I was ushered straight through to the studio which was much as we'd left it the previous evening, except his assistant was absent.

"I was hoping you could take his place today, Casey. He's indisposed, so I need this immense favor of you."

"I'd be more than honored to help out any way I can," I replied, unsure what was expected of me. I wasn't unsure for long.

"You will position the lights as I tell you, hand me the cameras as I ask, and you will take close-ups of…well, you will see."

I'm no prude but I do have to say that Truss's methods are unconventional. It's open to argument whether they are justified by the result. I understand now there is a certain sexual frisson that comes with the sorts of photographs Truss shoots but I was totally unprepared for the raw sexuality, and the extras I was asked to perform.

Truss makes his bread and butter money from commissions for classy advertising, fashion shoots, and so on, interspersing it with his artistic photographic sessions which end up on gallery walls. I almost begged off assisting him when I discovered this was one of his major artistic efforts. I was totally unprepared, especially to greet the model and get him settled.

Riz Massey was a god. Well, if he wasn't when he arrived, he would be by the time his photographs were hung on the walls of every major museum in the world. He made even Dallas look plain. In fact, he was so hot I started to worry about my oath of fidelity which was rather stupid because this guy was hardly likely to turn his lust on me. I was tongue-tied and awkward at first, until my professionalism kicked in and I repeated what would be expected of him during the shoot. It had all been explained to me in the hours before Riz turned up at the door around one o'clock.

"These guys never get out of bed before noon," Truss confided. "And I don't want them looking like they've spent the night drinking, drugging and whoring. You have to allow them a little latitude."

"Mr. Truss asked you to bring certain costumes," I said.

"In my bag," Riz replied as he began to shuck his street clothes.

I didn't know where to look so I busied myself with the lights, peeking at him from time to time because he didn't bother pulling the modesty panel closed. Considering what he was about to reveal to the camera, I guessed he had nothing to hide. He didn't.

He kept up a flow of conversation about his girlfriend who he was hoping to marry if this 'modeling gig' brought in enough cash. He had no idea who Truss was except he was 'some old dude who wants to take snapshots of my tackle.'

I was so affronted, I launched into a short history lesson of Truss's place in cultural history. When I ran out of breath, Riz whistled. "Shit, eh?" That was the impression I was after and then he went and ruined it, by adding, "If I'd known that, I would have asked for a bigger payment."

Riz might have had a cock that rivaled Jeff Stryker and a face that would stop a gaggle of queens in their tracks, but he had the finesse of a philistine.

Once the shoot got underway, I was so busy following Truss's shouted instructions I didn't have time to admire his technique or Riz's nudity, even when he got hard as stone. There was something about the soothingly hypnotic manner in which the photographer spoke that lulled both the model and me into a safe place, so that when Truss asked him to jerk his cock, the stud obeyed instantly. Truss went in for a close-up of his face while ordering me to grab another camera and get ready to take the extras.

Without prompting I knew he meant Riz's money shot and I was ready for the huge explosion of spunk that shot out of his achingly beautiful cock, spattering his abs like the paint sprays on a Jackson Pollock canvas.

I pulled back as Riz relaxed. Truss hadn't finished with him yet.

"Roll over on your stomach, Riz," Truss cooed and the young Adonis obeyed. "Pull your ass cheeks apart, Riz, show me that lovely moist hole of yours. Mm, that's it. Lovely. You really are a magnificent specimen. Arch your back, Riz. Yes, like that. Thrust your ass out, like you want the world to kiss it. To kiss your ring in worship."

I could not believe this straight stud was showing his sweet butthole in such a way it looked as if he wanted to be fucked senseless.

"Turn your head around, Riz, look over your shoulder. That's it, but keep your beautiful ass spread open. Wonderful. These photographs will make you famous, Riz. You'll have fame and fortune, more pussy than you'll ever have a chance to fuck."

I noticed Riz was hard again even after blowing a load a few minutes earlier.

"Just relax, Riz. Go with it. You feel the admiration of the world, adoring every part of your body, including your magnificent butt."

Truss beckoned for me to get ready as he dipped his fingers into the jar of grease he had at the side of the photographic set. He smoothed it into Riz's hole as he kept up the soothing banter. One, then two fingers disappeared into Riz.

I held my breath, mesmerized by what I was watching unfold. Truss unfastened the button on his casual trousers and they slipped effortlessly down his legs. He stepped out of them, totally naked from the waist down, his own cock oozing its appreciation of the nubile young man spread out before him. I gathered up his trousers, tossing them onto a nearby chair. I knew I needed to be ready for what occurred next.

Truss greased his cock and moved toward the vulnerable ass, nodding that I should go around to Riz's face, ready to shoot the pain of penetration. I kneeled to get the best shots I could although I knew these pictures would never be released to the public. I heard Riz groan as Truss entered his ass, watching the recognition dawn on his face, the pain flicker across him, then the resignation as Truss found that little knob of pleasure inside, massaging it with his cock

I often wondered what went through the minds of the models as an ugly old cuss like the photographer fucked their virgin holes. I suspect they were too far into the fantasy of wealth and fame to care. Or else he lulled them into such a sense of euphoria it was the only way the photo session could end.

Truss nodded that I should take shots from behind, so I got in for close-ups of his gnarled old cock plugging that sweet tanned ass, then back to Riz's face, with Truss leering behind him, as they both shot their loads at the same time.

Truss pulled out, flicked the excess spunk off his cock, retrieved his trousers and left the studio.

I went to fetch a warm wash cloth for Riz and when I returned he was lying on his back, his cock drooling, spunk all over his stomach and chest. I rubbed him clean without touching his cock, handing the cloth to him so he could finish up.

"You do it," he said lazily.

I held his cock as gently as possible and ran the flannel up and down the shaft which seemed to get him more excited. I squeezed the head to get the last remnants before rubbing it clean. I ran the cloth across his balls.

"That was so fuckin' intense," Riz said. "Is it always like that?"

"I'm just getting work experience," I said. "I've never been his assistant before."

"Gossip on the grapevine says he always does much the same every time. I swore I wouldn't let him go that far, but…"

"Yeah," I agreed. "It's his voice. Makes you want to do everything he says."

"Those pics…"

"No one will ever see them," I lied. "He uses them for a week or two then destroys them."

"I wouldn't mind a few for myself. If he can spare them."

"I'll ask for you. Here, you'll need to wipe…um… down there."

Riz lifted his legs in the air, parting his ass cheeks. "You finish me off, buddy."

I hesitated before rinsing the cloth and wiping down his crack, rubbing his hole, wondering whether I should push the cloth inside.

"That feels so good," Riz said, a real croak to his voice. "You want to have a go?"

I couldn't believe this sex god was asking me to fuck him. With the utmost reluctance, I shook my head.

"You're a gorgeous piece of man flesh and I'll probably live to regret this moment, but I have a boyfriend and we're totally monogamous."

"Hey, that's great," he said. "Sorry to tempt you. I don't think I'd have the willpower to turn down some chick if I was swabbing out her spooge riddled cunt and she asked me to have a go."

I swatted his butt to signify I'd finished.

"Thanks mate," he said as he went to get dressed.

By the time I'd cleaned up the set and turned off the lights, Riz was ready to leave. He'd already signed the release form and was waiting patiently for payment. The models all preferred cash so that they could hide it from tax. I had Riz sign the form to say he'd been paid, just a precaution in case he tried extortion later on, and penciled in an appointment for him to come over and look at the results of the session and chose one or two of the shots for his own collection. They would be worth a small fortune in a few years.

Riz patted me on the back. "Thanks mate. Don't be shy. If you see me in the street or in a bar, come on over, say hello."

"I will."

As I closed the studio door on him, I wondered if I'd live to regret not accepting his invitation to fuck that straight ass of his.

When I went back into the studio, Truss was waiting for me. "You turned him down."

I knew what he was referring to. "Of course, I did. I have a boyfriend—"

"Who won't let you fuck him—"

"Plus, I didn't think you'd like it."

"Why's that?"

"Because it's part of your mystique, the way you work. It's not exactly secret, but if I were to join in, it would be presumptuous, it would sully something beautiful that you've created."

"Not even a man as beautiful as Riz could tempt you?"

"Look, I won't say I wasn't flattered to be asked even though I know it was the residual of what you'd set up. And I won't say I wasn't tempted for a second or two, but I'm a professional. Just as there are a number of customers at the store I'd love to sock in the face, I don't. So, much as part of me would have loved to fuck Riz, especially because I don't get to indulge that part of my personality at home, I turned it off."

"How would you like this job permanently? I've had to dismiss that other incompetent fool. The job is yours if you want it."

"Your assistant?"

"Yes."

"For real?"

"Of course, for real. I'll pay more than you're getting in that shit job at the store. You'll have better working conditions. You'll be doing things you love while you hone your skills."

"When do I start?"

"You already have."

I could barely sit still at the computer as I downloaded the pics from the session, careful to keep his separate from the snaps I took.

I was to pick around six to eight of his and an equal number of mine so Truss could ascertain whether our thinking was similar. If not, he would train me. I also learned that he liked to have a nap immediately after the stress of a photo shoot. I was to wake him an hour later, and have my choices ready.

It took no time at all to choose the best of my shots. A miserable six in all and I was hard pressed to find a last one of sufficient quality. Not so, Truss's output. They were all superb and I agonized for the longest time before I narrowed the selection to eight magnificent portraits, all of which were worthy of museum space. Riz came up better than well.

I still had about twenty minutes to fill in so I thought I'd familiarize myself with the computer software he used. I was a novice and every little bit of practice would help. The most recent files were cluttered and messy, perhaps one of the reasons the latest assistant had not worked out. A quick glance at older files educated me to the manner in which Truss liked things stored and it would be easy to clean up the recent postings in much the same way.

I was down to the last file, pleased I'd managed to bring order to chaos. I clicked the unlabeled folder icon and a collection of jpg thumbnails popped up. I frowned;

the model looked familiar, too familiar, even at postage stamp size. Still, I needed to be sure. My stomach heaved as I opened one up to fill the screen. There before me was my boyfriend, his stiff cock straining in his hand, his eyes inviting the photographer to come and have his way with him.

Damian looked as shocked as I had felt on that awful day that I found my naked, and erect, boyfriend's photo on Lowell Truss's computer. Stefan had heard the story before and probably saw the pain did not get any less even with the passing of time. He leaned across the table at the trattoria and patted my hand.

"I'm sorry if it brings back bad memories," Damian said.

"I survived."

"That should have been in the film. Show Dallas up for the bastard he was."

"The documentary wasn't about me and Dallas, it was about Lowell Truss. We were collateral damage," I said. "Besides, finding that photograph was not anywhere near as bad as I believed at first."

A very attractive waiter interrupted the story and both Damian and I allowed Stefan to order for us – he was the expert in wines and the best dishes at the restaurant. The conversation became more general and less about Lowell Truss so I relaxed. So much, in fact, that Stefan took over the inquisition of poor Damian who seemed delighted that someone took an interest in him. I knew the young man was not Stefan's type so I had to assume he was doing it for me as I'm only inquisitive when I get behind a camera.

"He's just right for you," Stefan whispered when Damian took a lull in the conversation as an opportunity to go to the bathroom.

"I'm not looking for anyone," I shot back.

"Can't you see the synchronicity of this? You turn your back on your old life finally, by going to see that pile of shit that poses as a documentary about Truss but which is more to do with your dysfunctional relationship. It took you months to pluck up the courage to see it, so how did it feel?"

"It brought back painful memories but not so painful I couldn't shrug them off," I answered truthfully. "And I got hard. I think that's why a lot of people like the film. It's almost pornography. In my case, it is porn."

"So at that very same screening, you meet a cute young guy who is everything you need at the moment. He obviously adores you."

"Really? He keeps asking about Truss like all those twinks who think they're on to a good thing befriending me."

"Of course, I can't deny Truss comes into the story, how could he not? Damian is asking about you and your feelings."

"So he's a little more subtle how he goes about it. Christ, Stefan, he's an art student. He's probably in the toilet now texting all his friends to tell them what a coup he's had – he's at dinner with Casey McKinney."

"Wow, you have become cynical. I should sue Truss for alienation of affections. I really would like my old friend back."

"Come on, Stefan. I haven't changed. I just got more real."

"You should take Damian home and photograph him. You'll see what I mean. Then you should bugger the ass off him or beg him to fuck some sense into you."

The tension which threatened to break into an all-out brawl was interrupted by Damian's return. He sensed the change and, rather than sitting down again, he said, "Um…I've intruded enough on your night. I really appreciate the dinner, Stefan, I don't get to eat like that very often, or drink such amazing wine. I hope one day I can return the favor. Casey, it's been amazing meeting you in the flesh. You were my photographic hero before I saw the movie, now you're my real-life hero as well."

Suddenly, and unselfconsciously, he leaned down to kiss me on the cheek. I was speechless. He hurried out of the restaurant. I sat like a startled starfish while Stefan encouraged me to go after him. When I didn't, he did, pushing his way among the tables until he was out the door.

I finished off my wine as I waited for Stefan's return. I assumed he was coming back. When he did, he looked at me with such a disgusted look on my face, I had to react.

"What?"

He didn't answer. He merely threw some cash on the table, more than enough to pay for the meal, and told me he was taking me home.

I should have known. Damian was seated in the back seat of the car, awaiting our arrival.

Stefan shrugged. "He had no way of getting home. What was I supposed to do?"

"I'll catch a cab," I said. "Thanks for a lovely evening."

Stefan grabbed my arm, steering me toward his vehicle. "You'll do no such thing. Do you know how rude that would be?"

I allowed myself to be pushed into the front passenger's seat before Stefan got in and started the car. My apartment was about twenty minutes away, but I wasn't sure where Damian was staying.

A loud silence followed our departure and I scrambled through my brain for a topic of conversation. Stefan came to the rescue. "I'm just headed over to Casey's to shoot the breeze, why don't you come with us and have a look at his studio, see how he works, have a look at some of his unfamiliar photography?"

Damian was enthusiastic. "Wow, really? That would be so cool. I feel I've already taken up too much of your precious time, though."

"Nonsense," Stefan said. "Casey loves to show off."

I pinched Stefan's arm hard, hoping it would result in a bruise by the morning. If it's something I detest, it's showing someone my work and my studio.

The remainder of the journey Damian monopolized the conversation, keeping up a sickening display of enthusiasm and thanks. I was so close to screaming, 'Shut the fuck up' that I had to bite my tongue. This was just about the worst idea Stefan ever had.

It wasn't until we got inside my apartment that Damian's verbal diarrhea subsided to stunned awe. I suppose that would have been my reaction once upon a time, had I been taken to a famed photographer's lair. It was much my reaction when I first went to work for Lowell Truss.

"Ah, I see you've found the photos of your boyfriend," Truss said. He was looking over my shoulder as I worked at his computer. A little of the shock had worn off because I realized Dallas hadn't been in the old photographer's studios, these were my shots. His come-and-taste-my-cock look was for me, the photographer. It still didn't explain how they came to be on Truss's computer.

"Disregarding the model for a moment, the shots are very good indeed," Truss said. "Not up to my standard, but then who is?" He went on to point out a number of areas I could improve the composition but, basically, he was telling me I was worthy of his apprenticeship.

"How did you get the photos?" I asked when I could finally control my breathing. "These are absolutely private." Not so private, however, that Dallas hadn't pushed them on me to take as samples of my work when I first met Truss. I'd left them in the car. Deliberately.

"Not all that private if you go sending them everywhere. There's nothing to stop me sending them to my subscriber base, or to anyone else for that matter."

"I didn't send them," I raised my voice for emphasis. "Where did they come from?"

"Aha," he replied. He glided the mouse through a number of files to bring up the original email with attachment.

"I'll kill him," I said, for the email was from my own account. Dallas had obviously used my computer to further his own career after I'd specifically told him not to. "I'm really sorry. I don't expect you'll believe me, but I had nothing to do with this. In fact, I told him it would jeopardize my position with you."

"An ambitious young man?"

"Very." I sighed. "I've sorted through the pics you wanted me to choose. I also sorted out some of the mess left by your previous assistant. I'm sorry about this," nodding toward the computer. "I'll just get my things and go."

It had to be the shortest job I'd ever held.

"Easily fixed this time," he said, leaning across me to delete the email and the pictures of Dallas. "I believe that you had nothing to do with it because I saw the shocked expression on your face when you saw them. I'm not the most forgiving of men, Mr. McKinney. When you're famous…don't interrupt, I don't pay compliments lightly. I said, when you're famous, you'll learn to mistrust people's motives for befriending you. You never know if they are friends because they want to be or for what they can get out of you. You don't know if they want to fuck you because of you, or because of who you are. I'm at that age, I really don't care. As Gertrude Stein said, amazingly perceptively, 'A fuck is a fuck is a fuck.' Take it any way you can get it."

I hated to think I would ever become that cynical. Or that famous.

"Don't let that sort of thing happen again. You know my thinking on models." That was Truss's final word on the subject.

We spent the rest of the day going through my choice of photos of Riz.

Truss complimented me. "You've chosen well."

He listened as I told him my reasons for choosing each picture. Impressing him with my ability to put into words what he'd managed to capture on camera. We disagreed over a very small number and then it was time to leave.

"I'll see you in the morning, Casey," Truss said at the door. "I hope our little discussion earlier hasn't soured our relationship."

"Certainly not," I replied.

"Good. We'll start your training tomorrow. Have a pleasant evening."

It wasn't all that pleasant at first, as I tore strips off Dallas for his stupidity. I don't think he realized how serious his breach was. I had to scream to get some sense into his head. It wasn't until I said, "Had I been fired, you would have had to give up acting for a while and get a job to pay the rent until I could find one."

"Acting is my lifeblood," he wailed. "I couldn't give it up. It would be like lopping off a body part."

I was tempted to march into the kitchen and grab one of our large knives to hand to him to lop off the organ responsible for his second-favorite pastime.

"You think I should write and apologize, tell him it wasn't your fault."

"No," I shouted. "Don't under any circumstances contact him again. Look, I know why you did it, and I admire your attitude in attempting to get your career reignited, but as long as I'm there, he's out of bounds. I wouldn't want you to pose for him anyway now that I've seen what he gets up to."

Dallas made me spill the beans, insisting I describe Riz in pornographic detail. "He propositioned you?"

"Yes," I said, with a hint of pride in my voice.

"If he was half as hot as you describe, I don't know that I could have turned him down." When Dallas saw my frown of disapproval, he backed down. "Just an expression, I didn't mean it. You're all I need, baby." He sounded as sincere as a politician standing for re-election.

"Even had I wanted to, which I didn't," I emphasized, "It's a dismissible offence to Truss."

"Dirty bastard wants to keep them for himself."

I had to laugh and that broke the mood. Dallas was contrite for all of about five minutes. I wanted to ask 'What were you thinking sending him explicit photos like that?' but that scab was best left alone. Instead, I detailed Truss's dirty dealing with the incredible Riz. Dallas screwed his face up and uttered 'eww' so many times that I thought 'the lady doth protest too much.' However, I could see the light of opportunity go out in Dallas's eyes. I wouldn't have to worry about his pestering Lowell Truss again.

He also took me to bed and fucked the ass off me while I told him about Riz all over again. Yeah, I knew he was fantasizing and although he had his dick in me his mind was picturing someone else. It was okay, because it was Riz dicking me as far as my mind was concerned. Two can play at that game. Maybe I should invite him over.

From that day forth, Dallas liked to hear all about Truss's model photo shoots. He didn't care about the catalogue work or the fashion shoots because they didn't involve sex. A certain amount of fantasy helps spice up a relationship but it became such a constant with us that sometimes I didn't tell him when we did a model shoot, mainly because I was exhausted after one of those sessions – their intensity was debilitating so I knew why Truss took a nap afterwards. I admit I did save up those shoots I hadn't told Dallas about for occasions when my libido was in full force and his was a little sluggish.

His became even more sluggish as the months went by. His career stagnated to the extent he wasn't even being cast in the pretentious self-aggrandizing wanker productions, usually because 'grunge' was the new theatrical black, and a pretty boy like Dallas had no place in that sort of theatre. When I was a lowly shop assistant working behind the tie counter, our relationship was more or less equal, but now that I was thoroughly enjoying my position with Lowell Truss who was a generous teacher, I was thriving.

The black moods when Dallas was down began to impinge on the quality of our time together. I didn't mind supporting him and his burgeoning acting career, especially now that I was making a good wage, but it got my back up when I came home from work to a sink full of dirty dishes, clothes piling up because he hadn't bothered doing the laundry, to find him slobbing in front of daytime soaps on the TV.

My attempts to cheer him up failed monumentally; even the fantasies were having little effect on him. I invited friends over to help shake him out of his lethargy, and then I was inviting them over so I didn't have to talk to Dallas at all. He had taken to bar hopping during the day; I could smell it on his breath when I got home. At least he was home when I got in. I was thankful for small mercies.

I became quite close to Lowell Truss. I got to know him so well I could anticipate his next move so that he didn't have to constantly bark orders. I could adjust the lights to his satisfaction, I could make the models feel comfortable both before and after a session to the extent a few of them, such as Riz, became good friends.

Dallas and I had gone to Riz's wedding. He married a smashing woman who knew about his tryst with Truss and thought it a small price to pay for the wealth and fame it had brought. She even found it amusing that Riz held me in an iron grip when he declared, "If I was ever to turn gay, it would be for this man." Dallas was in a foul mood for about an hour afterwards.

With Truss's coaching, my photographs became thoroughly professional until one day, he said, "I can't teach you anymore. You are as near perfect as it's possible to be."

He could be that effusive because I was no competition in his area of expertise. I could never have reproduced the erotic tension he brought to the fore in every shoot. Okay, some were hotter than others, but that had to do with the co-operation of the model. The more co-operative, the better the shot. It was apparent who among the models baulked at following his instructions.

Truss's reputation became even more lustrous in the months leading up to his fiftieth birthday, especially when one of the city's major public galleries announced a major retrospective of his work, a kudos rarely offered to a living artist. Then came the news of the documentary.

"Show Damian your studio," Stefan suggested, making it sound as dirty as hell.

"I'm sure he's not interested," I said.

"Of course, I am," he smirked. "I'm very interested."

Oh oh.

To give him his due, he showed interest in the lay-out of my studio, my lights, my cameras…my everything.

"It's not at all like Lowell Truss's," he commented. "At least not from the picture of it we got in the film."

I had a few of my favorite shots adorning the walls, including the Dallas rampants, as I liked to call them.

"Wow," was all he said before moving on to others that were more my style. I had picked up a camera when we first entered, a habit of mine, and began snapping photos of Damian as he was engrossed in the pictures on the wall. He didn't notice because he was like a young gay boy at his first orgy: he didn't know where to turn his attention.

When Stefan called that the coffee was ready, we adjourned to the living room which was dominated by two large, framed Trusses; two pics which complemented each other and were among his most successful ever. One was of me. Not that I'd ever modeled for him.

"How can you bear to look at them every time you sit here?" Damian asked.

"I wonder the same thing," Stefan added.

"They're to remind me," I said.

"I'm not sure you need a constant reminder about that period of your life," Stefan said.

"Nothing has come close to replacing it."

Stefan was adamant. "Because you won't let it."

Damian interrupted. "I'm sorry, I didn't mean to start an argument."

"Casey and I have been having this conversation for so long we can do it in our sleep," Stefan joked. "Well, I must be off. Where can I drop you, Damian?"

He gave an address which, fortunately was on the way to Stefan's. That's why I was somewhat surprised when he said, "Totally opposite direction to the way I'm going and…" He made a show of thinking. "I know, why don't you stay here the night? I know Casey has plenty of room, and the two of you could get to know each other better."

My voice dripped venom when I said, "Why Stefan, if I didn't know better, I'd swear you were matchmaking and you don't even know if Damian has a boyfriend."

I felt like kicking him down the lift shaft, but he was too good a friend even with his interference.

A little too enthusiastically for my liking, Damian assured, "I don't. But I'm always on the look-out."

I escorted Stefan to the elevator.

"He's too good for you," he said.

"Just how did you come to that conclusion?"

"He's charming, erudite, keen to please, interested in photography."

I interrupted. "We don't know if he's a top or a bottom, whether he's into fisting or water sports…"

"I'm totally versatile, though I prefer to top. Not into the others, but I'm willing to learn if it's what you want," Damian yelled down the corridor. He was obviously eavesdropping on our conversation.

"Eager as a puppy," Stefan said as the elevator pinged on my floor. I kissed him goodbye and trudged back to my apartment. Damian, looking a little sheepish, was waiting for me.

"Thank you for a really wonderful day," he said. "When I went to the movies I never thought for a moment that I would spend an evening with one of my idols. I never thought you would be charming, and funny, and…hot. I know I'm not much to look at—"

"You are so wrong, Damian. Here, put your bag down, you're not going anywhere. You'll stay the night. I know you don't have money for a cab, and it's way too far to walk. To ensure you stay, I'm not lending you any money."

"Seriously?" He seemed particularly pleased with my outburst.

"It doesn't, however, mean we'll be rubbing body parts together."

He pouted theatrically, making me laugh.

"Come into the studio, I want to show you something."

During an intense discussion between Damian and Stefan about painter Francis Bacon earlier in the evening, I'd slipped away to download the shots I'd secretly taken of Damian. I cursed Stefan for always being correct: I really didn't notice people except through a camera.

"Close your eyes for just a moment, Damian."

He did as he was told and I clicked on the folder that contained his pictures, blowing up the one I thought best. "You can open them now."

He gasped. "Is…is that me?"

I nodded.

"You've made me beautiful," he said.

"No, I haven't," I corrected. "You are beautiful. I had to have a camera in front of me to see it for myself."

I'd captured something in his face that elevated it from the mundane into something extraordinary. He'd never stand out in a bar against all the beauties who flaunted their tantalizing wares, but for the connoisseur who was willing to dig below the surface, Damian was a catch worth the fishing.

I heard a convulsive sob and turned to see tears cascading down his face. "My mum always said I was beautiful. I never believed her. She said it came from inside. I thought it was bullshit. Well, you would. It's the sort of thing you'd tell your kid if he was homely, isn't it? Just maybe what she said is a little bit true."

He wiped his eyes with the back of his hands, hiccupping his tears away.

"I didn't mean to upset you," I said, embarrassed by such raw emotion, while the photographer inside me itched to capture the moment.

"Go on then," Damian said, attempting unsuccessfully to keep his emotions in check.

"You mean it?" I said, grabbing my camera without waiting for his reply.

Gasping for breath between his tears he brought on another attack of hiccups so that he was laughing while crying. It also meant he did not have the opportunity to pose or feel self-conscious. He looked so funny through the camera and his laugh was so infectious I broke up, too, scarcely able to control myself once I had captured all the pictures I wanted. I doubled over and

Damian grabbed my camera before I dropped it. Suddenly the subject and the photographer were reversed and he was taking shots of me almost rolling on the floor.

Eventually, we both sat on the studio floor side by side wiping tears of laughter from our cheeks.

I asked him, "How did you know I wanted to take a photo of your tears?"

"It's what any great photographer would want to do," he said simply.

That deserved a kiss. What I probably didn't deserve was the warmth with which he responded. I was tired of performing for one-night stands who were fucking me for my celebrity. I had come to appreciate what Lowell Truss had warned me came with the territory. I felt comfortable with Damian even though I'd known him less than a day.

"I want so much to make love to you, Casey, if you'll let me," he said gently.

When was the last time someone said they wanted to make love to me?

That's what it was: leisurely, sensual lovemaking, not the frantic rutting I was used to. I let Damian take control, and he must have licked every square inch of my body, including my ass. My body tingled as he lifted my legs onto his shoulders in order to guide his cock into my twitching hole. His body was firm and muscled without the definition of a gym bunny or a steroid addict, his cock a comfortable size that would never get him an appearance in a porn movie. That suited me just fine.

He sure knew what he was doing when it came to pleasure and he rode me gently but firmly until I was begging him to bring me off. He'd brought me to the edge so many times, only to pull me back from the brink at the last moment, it was threatening to turn my balls blue. He wouldn't let me touch myself, so when he finally wrapped his fist around my cock to pump me as he rammed his cock into my gaping ass, I shot a load like a fountain as I felt his spunk flood my guts.

I was awash with perspiration but too exhausted to get out of bed. We fell asleep, Damian cradling me in his arms. Seemed so odd at first, the older man cradled by the twink. In no time at all, it seemed the most natural thing in the world.

Working with Truss as his assistant, I became inured to his use of sex to get the results that he wanted. His sexual activity was really no more than another prop to his photographic arsenal. I may not have approved but when it came to great art, I tucked my morality out of sight. So when the idea of the documentary film was mooted, I thought he'd turn it down, especially as it was to culminate in unprecedented access to one of his model photo shoots. They were the most holy of holies. I had to sign a non-disclosure clause when I first started working for him, although it was obvious the models would blab. As there was never any 'official' acknowledgement of what went on in the studio between artist and model, Truss could pretend it didn't happen. To have a film crew on site was courting the public's opprobrium and the scorn of his colleagues. I advised him against it.

"The documentary is a wonderful tribute, but it's better to tease than reveal all," I said.

"I've always been a divisive figure, a controversial artist. I've been banned, attacked in the press, you name it. Why not give them one big 'fuck you'?"

I couldn't think of a reason not to if that's what he wanted to do.

"I have to consider you in this, Casey. It will involve you almost as much as me. You'll be seen as condoning my actions. I know you don't totally approve, but you excuse it on the grounds that I produce great works of art. That's dangerous. Where do you draw the line? Is any behavior acceptable if great art is the outcome?"

"I think behavior has to be guided by the legal system," I answered, realizing how naïve that sounded as soon as it left my lips.

"Let's leave the argument to philosophers and Bible bashers," he said. "What you must do is decide whether you wish to be part of the film just as you've been such an integral part of my life and career these past few years. If you do appear, I can't say that you will escape any of the backlash that I may endure, but it will lift your profile. Again, I can't guarantee that your career will be given the boost that, say, a model will receive…"

"Of course, I'll do it," I said, "Not for the reasons you list, but because I want to be there for you."

Truss hated cheap sentiment, so he merely nodded his thanks. As he moved away, I added, "You'll need a good model, the best you can find, although not so good he pulls focus."

I thought I heard him sigh.

That evening, when I told Dallas of the documentary, without mentioning I would be part of it lest he get jealous, he said bitterly, "Who wants to watch that old wanker making his porn photos?"

"A lot of people," I said, irritated by his negativity. "The model will probably be able to ask any price for his talent afterwards."

"They're not going to show the old cunt fucking the model up the ass?"

"Not unless they want an X rating, but there are ways to imply that without showing it in close-up. That's tantalizing without showing the money shot."

"You mean," he said, "the audience won't know for sure what's going on?"

"I think they'll have a fair idea but there won't be any proof on screen."

"Hmmm."

"Don't even go there," I warned. "I am not putting your name forward; I told you he doesn't work that way. He has to discover the model for himself. And like I'm going to dangle my boyfriend for him to fuck when that same boyfriend won't give his ass up to me."

"I don't take it in the ass, you know that."

"I hate to tell you that's the secret of his artistic success."

I knew Dallas didn't have a hope at the gig, but I did love taunting him with the prospect of the chosen model being the darling of the international artistic jet set.

"Yeah, well, he's never getting his dick in my butt."

"You know, there's a lot of planning and shit to pull this off smoothly so it may mean a bit of after-hours—"

"No problem, honey," he said, using an endearment I loathe. "My good news is that I got an acting job. If it's successful, there's the option to move the production to a larger theatre."

"That is such good news," I gushed. I really was pleased for him. "Tell me all about it."

I couldn't help but feel his enthusiasm. It was the lead role in an important new play by one of the most sought after up-and-coming cutting edge playwrights. He would have to change his hair coloring and style and…I hadn't seen Dallas this excited in almost a year. I was glad to have my old lover back. That night we celebrated in the best way possible.

The documentary crew was amazingly unobtrusive even as they filmed Lowell's daily routine. I kept to the background as much as possible, not because I'd been asked to but in deference to the subject of the documentary. The director, who went by the name of Ced, was around Truss's own age, a pipe and slippers type who wore leather patches on his tweed sports coat. He was obviously gay and I thought a bit of a voyeur which I suppose most filmmakers are, although he encouraged Lowell into the most lascivious of admissions which I didn't always think appropriate. I suppose, I thought him a bit of a sleaze. The sound man and the cameraman were about my age and thoroughly professional. Both were cute in a straight sort of way, but no world beaters.

I got so used to them, they became part of the furniture. However, Truss always seemed acutely aware of their presence, playing to the camera like an ageing diva. I heard him pontificate – it's the only word that springs to mind – during interviews, giving pretentious justifications for what he did and discussing photography in such vomitus arty farty terms, he was coming across as a prize twat. That was his concern; mine was to ensure everything ran smoothly, especially as the 'big day' was fast approaching. I didn't want to add to Lowell's stress by asking if he'd chosen a model but, sensing my concern, he put my mind at rest. The model's name was Mario.

My hours became erratic, as did Dallas's, but we used every moment when our paths crossed to update each other on our progress. I was genuinely excited for him and his new hair gave him an air of authority and danger that I liked. I told him so and he buggered me into the living room floor as a reward. Punishment? It did actually feel like that at times. I wondered whether I was experiencing his character vicariously. He certainly exuded a new confidence he'd so sadly lacked of late.

On the morning of Lowell Truss's big day, I was more nervous than him. Dallas was still asleep when I left home earlier than usual that morning because I wanted the day to be perfect. Lowell was up, double checking his cameras, a task he normally left to me. I wasn't insulted because everything had to go like clockwork. He warned me that he may make extra requests today just so I could share some camera time and because he was going to attempt something new. I didn't think this was really the time for a change of direction.

"Trust me," he said. "Today is my gift to you."

I had no idea what he meant but that was the least of my worries. Roy, the cameraman, and Leon, the sound guy, would film and record me as a bit of background while I set up. The filming would begin in earnest when I welcomed the model. Ced wanted Lowell to do that but he refused, arguing it was always the assistant's responsibility and everyone knew that. If he were to start faking, he believed it would make the whole documentary bogus.

Set-up was painless and over too quickly for the camera, so I had to repeat it. That was okay as I had time to fill in. I made the guys coffee and a snack from Lowell's kitchen because I knew the photo shoot would be intense and there would be no stopping. Both Truss and I had stressed that there would be no stop/start during the model shoot. I was surprised Ced didn't hire a second cameraman – just in case. I guess the budget didn't stretch to such a luxury.

We practiced my opening the door to greet the model but, in the end, it was decided to follow him up the path upon his arrival, revealing me at the door when I opened it. They were shooting many hours more than was required and I suspected a lot of me would end up on the cutting room floor, or whatever the digital equivalent is these days.

I went to ensure Lowell was in a good frame of mind and found him whistling.

"This is it," he smiled. "No backing out now. No chance of doing it again because they have to have the film ready in a matter of weeks because it's the centerpiece of the official birthday celebrations. I know they've been editing the early sections already."

Today's escapades were the culmination of the documentary, and its final scenes.

"You'll be magnificent," I said.

"Don't forget today is as much for you as it is for me."

It was nice of him to say so, but I didn't believe it.

I went into the studio, took a deep breath and heard the director on his mobile. "In position, please, Casey. They're on approach."

I'd memorized all the necessary information about Mario, today's model, to put him at his ease. From his CV photograph, he was certainly a looker with a body that would be the envy of most gay boys. I just hoped his personality was as pleasant.

I stood at the end of the hallway, awaiting Ced's signal. The door chimed, Ced gave me the go ahead, and I walked down the hallway to open the door, my best smile pasted on my face. It didn't stay pasted for long. Today's model was…Dallas.

"What are you doing here?" I hissed.

Dallas smiled, replying in his normal voice. "I'm here to model for Mr. Truss. My name is Dallas."

I heard the director muttering, "I thought we were expecting a Mario."

"You won't get away with this," I said between clenched teeth.

"I already have. Today's model is lying in a hospital bed after an unfortunate fall down some stairs while pissed as a fart."

We were standing in the doorway hissing like two gay snakes when Ced screamed, "Cut."

I stormed into the studio with the others bringing up the rear. How could I possibly explain this to Lowell? He'd think I'd planned it. I slammed into the main house to explain the situation, telling the film crew to stay where they were.

Truss already knew, he was steaming when I found him, balling and unballing his fists.

"I don't expect you will believe me, but I had nothing to do with this, I swear."

"That is of little consequence now. I need calm to rethink my concept. Leave me. Have him sign the release. Tell Ced I will be in presently."

"You can't go ahead using Dallas."

"Why not?" Truss asked.

"He's my boyfriend." I thought that a reasonable argument.

"So?"

"You fuck the models. Or have you forgotten?"

"I haven't. Has your boyfriend? I presume you have discussed what goes on here with him."

"Of course."

"And he's turned up of his own free will, has he not?"

"Yes."

"We're all adults. He's an attractive young man. You're a professional. What else is there to say? Go and prepare."

Too shocked to argue, I returned to the studio. I dragged Dallas to the small desk I used for the models to sign their waiver agreement.

"What the fuck are you doing here?" I snarled. "Just get out of here and go home."

He smiled in such a patronizing manner I wanted to slug him. "What's it look like I'm doing? I'm posing for the man who is going to get me the career I deserve and which I've had no luck in getting on my talent alone."

"After what I told you about him?"

"I'm sure you exaggerated," he said. "You just couldn't bear the idea that I might become more famous than you?"

"If I thought I would ever be jealous of a boyfriend, I would have settled down with an accountant." I took deep breaths to control my heart; it was thumping so wildly it threatened to burst through my chest wall. "Just for the record, I did not exaggerate. If anything, I downplayed just how sleazy Lowell Truss is."

"If he's as bad as you say, how come he gets some of the most beautiful men in the world to pose for him? Straight men?"

"They're men who will do anything to have Lowell Truss photograph them because they know it will increase their profile and they'll have job offers from all over."

Dallas looked superior. "Exactly."

"Weren't you the one who was adamant our relationship had to be monogamous or it was all over?"

"Yeah, and it still applies."

I was totally exasperated. "Don't you realize the secret of Lowell Truss's success is that he fucks every model in the ass? That's how he gets those incredible shots."

"Well, he won't be fucking me!"

"You want a dollar for every model I heard say that? I wouldn't have to work. He talks them into it. Plus, if you don't do what he says, then there's no photo shoot. No career. No success. A couple of guys tried it. Truss threw them out. When they came back a few weeks later, their assholes greased, ready to be used any way he wanted, he closed the door in their face. He doesn't take rejection kindly."

"Who gives a shit, Casey? I have no career, no prospects, no future. This is my last chance."

"What about…oh no, there is no play, is there? It was all a fiction."

"Give the man a cigar," he sneered. "I've spent the last two months shadowing Truss's every movement. Watching him as he tracked down the perfect model. I put myself in his path so many times he was forced to consider me although I could see he thought he knew me but couldn't place who I was."

"That's why you changed your look."

"Uh huh. In the end, it didn't work the way I hoped. He chose this jumped up wannabe. Mario."

"So you got him drunk and pushed him down some stairs."

"I may have encouraged him a little."

Truss strode into the studio, the film crew capturing his grand entrance. He made an ostentatious examination of his cameras before coming over to the desk where Dallas had signed his release.

"Is there a problem?" he said.

"I can't do this, Lowell?"

"Why not? Are you ill?"

"You know why not."

"You're a professional, Casey. As such, I expect you to behave as you always do. Understood? You will do exactly as I tell you."

I relented. "Understood." I couldn't let him down after all he'd done for me.

"Good, now let's get this over and done with. You understand what's in store, Dallas?"

"I think so."

Truss clapped his hands and we were off.

The initial photos of Dallas as he slowly peeled off each item of clothing while Truss snapped dozens of shots would be superb. I had an eye for it now, and forgetting for the moment it was my boyfriend I was watching, maybe it would all work out for the best. Maybe Truss would not go all the way, in deference to our friendship.

Finally, Dallas was naked, his cock a beautiful sight. I heard admiring whispers from Roy and Leon. My boyfriend was stroking his cock leisurely, a look of bliss on his face. Don't let anyone tell you it's easy. It's not. It's exhausting work for the model as well as the photographer and his assistant.

I saw that dreamy look on Dallas's face that's the cornerstone of the Lowell Truss photographic portrait. The cameraman went in for a close-up.

"Are you feeling comfortable, Dallas?" Truss asked quietly.

"Mmm," he murmured.

"Are you feeling sexy, Dallas?"

"Yeah."

"Show me how sexy, Dallas."

He licked his lips, squeezing one of his solid pecs, as he milked his cock. I almost blew in my trousers. I could never produce shots like this. Roy was hard in his tight-fitting shorts and I was pretty sure I could see a solid ridge in Leon's jeans.

"Turn over, Dallas. Show us your sexy ass," Truss commanded.

Without a single hesitation, Dallas rolled onto his stomach, reaching back to pull his cheeks apart with his hands, gazing back over his shoulder at the camera.

"That's a beautiful hole you have there, Dallas. Does it feel sexy when I touch you there?"

Truss ran his finger along Dallas's ass crack, hesitating at the hole before pushing into the sphincter.

"Oh, God."

"You like that, Dallas?"

"Mmm, yeah. That's hot."

"Casey tells me you don't like anything in your asshole, is that true?"

"Usually," he purred.

"So what's the difference?"

"You're good for my career, Casey isn't."

"You mean you'll endure anything in exchange for fame and fortune, Dallas?"

"You got it," my boyfriend said, wriggling his ass around Truss's thumb.

"So, you're a whore, Dallas?"

"If that's what it takes."

He turned to look straight at me, his face contorted with pleasure at his success, daring me to interrupt him taking pleasure from a man he despised fingering his ass.

"You like being a whore, Dallas?"

"If it gets me what I want."

Roy focused on Dallas's face as he dreamily admitted to whoring his body for a chance at the success that had so far eluded him. It's the most honest I had ever heard him

"Unzip the cameraman, Casey."

"What?"

"Don't play dumb. You've been my assistant long enough to know when I say something you snap to it. Now, unzip the cameraman."

Roy seemed as surprised as I was but made no attempt to stop me as I slid the zip to his shorts down.

"Take them off him, Casey. That's it, pull them down. And his briefs."

Roy's cock was a thick sausage, uncut and already moist at the head.

"Now guide it to Dallas's mouth."

I was on autopilot, telling my brain this was just another model shoot and not my boyfriend about to be buggered on the studio set. Roy's cock twitched in my hand as I moved it toward Dallas's mouth. He opened up in anticipation, wetting his lips before his tongue snaked out to lick the excess cream from the slit.

"All the way in, Casey."

I helped Roy slide his cock into Dallas's craw, secretly pleased when he gagged. He hated giving oral, contenting himself with being blown, never reciprocating for me.

"That's it, Dallas, suck that big hard prick. You like sucking cock, boy?"

"Mmm," was all he could manage, Roy filming his efforts from above.

"Shit, that's so hot," Roy admitted.

"Grab your camera, Casey."

I knew what that meant. My heart almost stopped. The pit of my stomach felt like it does when the roller coaster drops. I was afraid I might puke.

I did as instructed. What else could I do? Storm out? That would achieve nothing. I'd already learned a valuable lesson about my boyfriend today. Perhaps, there were more eye openers on the way.

Truss had already greased Dallas's hole and his own cock while I'd been busy with Roy. I had my camera. I was being forced to take graphic close-ups of my boss fucking my boyfriend in his virginal butt. That was my job.

"Put my cock in your boyfriend's ass, Casey."

I had never been asked to perform that duty before. Truss was attempting to humiliate me. What made it worse was that it was being filmed for posterity.

"Hold on to my cock, Casey. Guide it in. He's never been fucked before. But he'll let an ugly old faggot like me have his ass because I can do things for him whereas you can do nothing. No ass for you, Casey, even though he's your boyfriend."

I took my hand off his gnarled old cock and he pushed it straight in.

"My god, you're so tight. You really are a virgin."

Truss rammed until his cock was balls deep in my boyfriend's ass. Dallas twitched in pain but Roy's cock kept him from screaming. Truss began his fucking action and I was there to watch every moment through the camera. I knew what he wanted and I did it, hating every moment of it. My tears threatening to overflow.

Truss was particularly brutal that afternoon, caring little for the model's discomfort. While part of me was pleased Dallas was in pain, another part of me hurt for him.

"Shit, I'm gonna come soon," Roy said.

Truss slowed down. "Pull your cock out, I want to see your spunk all over his face. Okay. Get your camera ready, Casey."

I moved into position, relieved I no longer had to watch Dallas being buggered.

"Open your mouth but don't you dare swallow, Dallas," Truss commanded. "Keep it on your tongue. Show us what's in your mouth while your boyfriend photographs it. Understand."

Dallas nodded. Roy pulled his cock out, jerking it as best he could while filming. I caught the first spasm as the spunk flew across Dallas's face, degrading his beauty. The next shot in his mouth, the third spattered against his cheek. The spunk ran down his face as I moved in for a close-up. Dallas smiled at me as he swirled the cum around on his tongue, poking it out so I could get a good shot of his degradation.

"You ready for more whoring, Dallas?"

"Anything you say, Lowell."

"I'm gonna breed your ass, son. Fill your ass with my cum. Fuck you in front of your boyfriend. What do you think of that?"

"Make me your total cock slut, your faggot boy. Fuck me till I'm full of spooge."

"Oh, we'll do that all right, boy."

I handed Truss his camera.

"Look at me," Truss said.

Dallas turned to look over his shoulder, his face sex-smudged in Truss's patented style. No one could withstand him.

"Look at your boyfriend, Dallas. Tell him what you're feeling. Do it."

Dallas turned to me, his face an evil sneer. I watched it through the camera, seeing my boyfriend for the first time, the veneer stripped away.

"I fuckin' love your cock in my ass, Lowell. It feels so good; you could fuck me to death. I want to drink your cum and your piss."

"You will. Boy, have no doubt about that."

"I'll do anything to be famous. I'll be your fuckhole, your toilet, whatever you desire."

Dallas kept it up, all the while staring straight at me his face running with spunk, Truss fucking his ass savagely. Finally, Truss bellowed and shot his cum into Dallas's ass. He pumped a few times before pulling out, moving around to Dallas's mouth to have him suck his cock clean.

"He's all yours, boys," Truss called as he went into the house for his nap. "You just keep shooting, Casey. I want to see the highlights when I get up."

"Keep the camera rolling, Roy. I think we'll make a fortune selling the X-rated version of the documentary on the net." The repulsive Ced had his clothes off and his cock in Dallas's ass before I even knew what was going on. Leon was about to impale Dallas's mouth.

I endured it all. Dallas gave the performance of his life, except that I never believed for a moment it was a performance. It was all too real. They took turns fucking his ass and his mouth, covering him with cum and piss until I thought he'd yell, 'no more.' Instead he encouraged them to take all sorts of degrading liberties with his body. I did the best I could, recording my boyfriend's total capitulation to the dark side, tears pouring down my face. Tears for lost innocence. Tears for the end of our relationship. Tears for the betrayal of two people I trusted.

It was those tears that became the defining portrait of that final shoot. It was the last Lowell Truss ever did. He had sneaked back into the studio and snapped away as I blubbered my life away. But it was his life, in reality that was ebbing. He'd known that all along.

In the end, I had to forgive him. He made me famous. The photograph, *Casey, with Tears,* was the last iconic picture he took. It became famous. It appeared on the posters for the documentary. When the film itself appeared, I became even more famous: the wronged lover.

The film was as controversial as Lowell wanted, generating extensive debate in cultural circles as to what is permissible to achieve great art. I had no problem being employed by many of the people and companies that had previously employed Lowell Truss. I visited him often, once I found out about his illness. He had a particularly virulent strain of cancer, announcing his retirement to fight the disease, at the movie's launch.

There are still hopes he'll return to work, producing even better iconic portraits. There are still lines of models sending their shots and CVs in wild hope. I suspect it's all in vain. But illness has not stilled his tongue. Nor has it prevented people attempting to get to the now reclusive photographer through me by feigning friendship.

"That Dallas guy was a dick," he said one afternoon when I was attempting to spoon feed him some liquid which was posing as soup. "You're better off without him. He's jealous, shallow and not a particularly good fuck."

"Well, I'll never know, will I?"

"You could have had a turn when the other guys had finished with him."

"Eww," I laughed. "Besides, it's forbidden in my job description."

"See, always the consummate professional."

Suddenly, I was in demand. Lowell had chosen his favorite images from the shoot and left it to me to print them. Of the two best, and I would have chosen them myself, one was of Dallas looking like lust incarnate, his face covered with a string of Lowell Truss's life force. The other was of me, a true professional going about his task even though his heart was being torn apart, my face awash with tears. They were the two photographs I chose for my living room wall – to remind me.

To remind me that fame and fortune are strange bedfellows. Dallas got his in the end. Literally. Though not as he expected. The documentary opened up an exciting new career direction for him. He's appeared on countless magazine covers, DVD slicks, in interviews. His name is known worldwide. He's now the most famous gangbang bottom in gay porn history. His ass has been immortalized in rubber. Yeah, I fucked it once when someone told me it was just like fucking Dallas himself. If that's the case, then I haven't missed much.

During the night, I awoke with a raging appetite. Where once I would have scurried off to the bathroom to relieve myself, this time Damian gave himself willingly. He was miles better than any cast rubber reproduction of Dallas. I made a note to send Stefan a case of his favorite wine in the morning. I worried that this feeling would last just one night. I hoped for more, but Damian was young. Even if it was a one-night stand, I was determined now that bitterness and cynicism would not prevent my seeking another mate.

Damian was perfect, though. I don't know why I hadn't seen that for myself. I snuggled closer and fell asleep. In the morning, I awoke alone. I hoped, but Damian wasn't in the kitchen preparing coffee. He was gone. His bag was gone too, so he wasn't out doing something romantic like buying croissants. All that lingered was the smell of him in the pillow. I breathed in his scent hoping it might bring him back, but I was a realist now.

I wandered into the living room to sip the coffee I made myself, while I thought back over the previous day, wondering whether the young man would sign a release form so I could distribute the amazing photos I'd taken of him.

It was time to take down the pictures that had hung on my living room wall like an albatross. When I looked up, I realized they were already gone. Replaced. Sometime during the night, while I slept, Damian had taken the pictures off the wall, probably storing them in my studio, and had chosen two pictures from the day before. He'd printed them and stuck them to my wall as replacements. Instead of my teary portrait, there was one of me smiling like I'd never smiled before, looking across a short expanse of wall at a beautiful photo of Damian. On it, he had drawn a speech balloon which read: "I know it's early days but I have feelings for you. Care to see what develops?" Under that was his phone number.

Once upon a time, I would have played games, left it a few days, played it cool. Not today. I picked up the phone and dialed his number.

"Hey," I said when he answered.

Middle Man for Madame Blavatsky

Steven was like a kid with two new toys. "I want to be fucked both ends at once like a human kebab."

For two guys in their early forties, this was an invitation from the gods, especially as the guy issuing the invitation was a twink with the sex appeal of the hottest Hollywood hunk only ten times more available. And all because of the occult.

There's a lot of bullshit talked about the occult. How do I know? Simple really. Whenever the coffers run a little low and I need money to pay the utility bills or for some little luxury the long-term bf covets, I stick out the shingle that reads "Tarot Readings to the Gay Gentry" and wait for the loot to roll in. Don't run away with the idea that I'm not legit. Over the years, I discovered a certain affinity for reading the cards and most of my clients go away happy or, in a few cases, relieved.

The first time I advertised in the gay press I was inundated with requests – for readings – the questions most men wanted answering concerned sex. Or the variations thereupon, such as relationships, wealth, or the body beautiful. No one ever, not once, asked about world peace or the cure for cancer.

Whether it was about the boyfriend, one-night stands or the likelihood of bedding that hunky barman, it all boiled down to that little piece of flesh dangling between their legs or that little puckered hole wedged snugly between their butt cheeks. And in a small percentage of the cases, that little piece of flesh got hard, or that little puckered hole got the itch, and I found myself servicing the bits in question.

Not long ago the spiritual urge took over once again, the DVD player went on the fritz, so out came the Aleister Crowley tarot cards, and out went the flyers and advertisements. Unbeknown to me, the occult was about to put a little spice back into my fifteen-year relationship with Warwick, my significant other. Don't be a smart ass, of course I couldn't see it coming, I can read people, I can't foretell the future.

Let's face it, if you have to consult me about a relationship or your chances with a certain gym dandy, you have a snowball's chance in hell because what you should be doing is getting out there and doing it, not sitting back passively consulting bits of colored cardboard. Can anyone say the word 'loser'?

Steven sounded like all the other typical clients when he rang for an appointment although far too young to be suffering the relationship battle fatigue of middle-aged gay men. Most asked simple questions such as 'How much?' 'How long?' or 'Can I tape it?' Steven asked more penetrating questions such as 'How old are you? Do you have a partner? Do you live with him? How long have you been together?'

I was about to fob him off with the 'none of your business' response I have when people get too personal but he sounded so sexy I curbed my tongue and answered him truthfully, thinking the worst he could do is waste my time. To my surprise, he made a booking even when I told him the truth that we were probably the same age as his parents. I was even more surprised when he turned up, somewhat early, for his appointment.

"Himbo," Warwick whispered as he brought him into the makeshift tarot room, our living room but with the lights dimmed and the curtains pulled, the jasmine and patchouli incense lending a slightly decadent air to the proceedings. Rather than a psychiatrist's lounge, which would have been the most appropriate piece of furniture for most of my visitors, or a conventional table and chairs, I lay the cards on a multi-colored silk cloth spread over the coffee table while seated on the floor. My customer would perch on a comfortable cushion opposite me to shuffle and cut the cards. Warwick played no part in the proceedings other than to usher the client in then he disappeared to watch TV in the bedroom upstairs.

Steven was tall, blond, skinny, and with a terrible, terrible problem. Or so he said. He was young and had an older lover – by older he meant mid-thirties. The lover was cute, filthy rich...and possessive. But that information came out only much later.

I usually chatted to my clients, especially on their initial visit, to calm their nerves and see if I could ascertain what they wished to consult me about. Tarot readers are the opposite of bar staff, priests, and sex workers who listen to people's woes and life stories, nodding sagely, offering relief with alcohol, forgiveness, or sex. We card readers listen to problems, nod our heads, and usually tell them what they want to hear so they go away elated, although sometimes we have to be cruel to be kind. It's no use inflating the impossible dream when you sense there is no happy ending. We're not like clairvoyants who offer hope of a hereafter to bereaved relatives or lovers.

Watching Steven cross his legs under the coffee table opposite me, he looked eager as a puppy, far from distressed. In fact, I'd never seen a more confident and endearing young man. I wondered if it were a trap of some sort, a newspaper exposé of ageing gay tarot readers preying on young and impressionable young men. Or perhaps a joke by one of my erstwhile friends, or an enemy, to make me look foolish.

He handed the cards back and as I lay them out, he watched with interest but none of the chatter that normally accompanied the process, particularly by people who shuddered at the more grisly cards without understanding their significance. He'd chosen *The Knight of Cups* as the card that most represented himself: romantic, confident, artistic, and welcoming of new experiences. It seemed to fit him perfectly. If he had a conundrum, it had nothing to do with romance. I had never seen so many propitious cards for such a young man. "You don't have romantic problems. You're already in a relationship which pleases you. Money is not a problem. You're young and healthy. You have a rosy future ahead of you. So we must look elsewhere for the reason you wish to consult the cards."

I'd had a few men who'd turned up for a reading whose sole purpose had been for sex, seeing my fee as a payment for a fuck. They were invariably disappointed and their fee was promptly refunded. If sex grew out of mutual attraction during a reading, I was more than happy to oblige although I usually made it for a future date. That way, neither of us felt exploited.

"Happy as it is, there is something missing in your relationship," I said.

He nodded imperceptibly. He wasn't one of those people who sat, arms crossed over their chest, smugly refusing to engage in any way, goading me to tell them their problem from the cards alone. It was usually easy but wasted a great deal of time and they felt cheated when their session wound up with little headway made on a solution.

Steven was not like that, he'd volunteered a certain amount of information and now, cognizant of what he'd asked during his phone booking, I made one of those fortuitous stabs in the dark.

"I see a minor problem with your love life," I said warily but knew I was on the right trail when he sat up straighter paying rapt attention to every word. "Your lover is somewhat staid in his ways; I suspect he's a top." Again, the automatic head bob that I was sure even Steven didn't know he was making in agreement.

"You find playing the same role repeatedly somewhat…unfulfilling. Sometimes you'd like to bust loose and change the ritual. The main source of your frustration is…" I took a deep breath before continuing, hoping that I was correct, "…a lack of multiple orgasms." He looked deflated by my euphemism. Perhaps he didn't understand, as I'd skirted the issue.

"Sorry to generalize. Your discontent is caused by group sex. The lack of it."

"Right on!" Steven yelled. "God, you're good." If only my lovers had expressed their appreciation of my sexual prowess with such enthusiasm.

"Your boyfriend is too possessive for you to suggest it. He is too insecure as yet to trust your affection for him. Given time, he will come around although you will only indulge on those occasions where it occurs spontaneously. You will never plan such an eventuality. And you will both be happy in the results and learn to trust each other."

"How about it, then?" he asked, enthusiastically.

"How about what?"

"A threesome. With your mate upstairs?"

I knew Warwick would be in it like the proverbial rat up the proverbial drainpipe. I sighed.

"Is that a 'yes'?" Steven asked eagerly.

"Of course it is," Warwick shouted from the top of the stairs where he'd been listening all along.

"Great!" Before I had a chance to move from psychic to sexual mode, Steven had all his clothes off. By the time he reached the bottom of the stairs, so had Warwick.

It was left to me to get the towels, the condoms and the lube and when I got back Warwick was seated on the coffee table, Steven slurping on his cock.

I stripped to join them. Steven's hairy blond ass was bobbing free so I kneeled on the carpet to rim his funky butt crack, licking and swirling my tongue in his luscious hole. He took time out from Warwick's rather substantial dick, which was dripping pre-cum and saliva, to announce, "I want to be fucked both ends at once like a human kebab."That would be no trouble at all.

I was sucking and chewing on Steven's hot, wet hole, priming it for Warwick's cock, once our visitor had finished deep throating it with such skill Warwick was groaning in that manner which meant he was about to lose it.

From the taste of Steven's swollen butthole, I knew he was craving cock and as my tongue was no match for Warwick's throbber, I gracefully gave way. I ripped open the condom packet with my teeth before I joined Steven, taking turns at slurping on Warwick's spit-soaked prick. During a brief lull in the oral maneuverings, I slipped the rubber over his cock, nodding that he should take care of a little anal business. As Warwick loved nothing better than gaping twink ass, he moved quickly to kneel behind our visitor, adding a little lube to my spit, and lined up his cock with the inviting hole.

I'd managed to insinuate myself onto the coffee table to take his place in order to pull Steven's face down onto my cock. I watched as he buried his lips down to my balls, licking the underside of my shaft as his head nodded like he was bobbing for apples.

There was a slight muffled yelp of pain when Warwick breached his ass, Steven hesitating mid-suck, his eyes opening wide, to absorb the pain before Warwick thrust harder still. I guessed it was the sense of euphoria that caused a smile that began with slight curls at the corners of Steven's lips until it spread, lighting up his entire face.

"Slut fuck me, guys. I wanna feel every inch." His voice was hoarse, heavy with expectation. The last thing we wanted to do was disappoint him.

I watched Steven taking my cock in and out of his cute little cocksucking mouth, the shaft pushed down by Warwick's battering of his rear. I pulled his face up and planted a kiss on those swollen lips but he seemed more interested in getting his mouth back around my cock than tongue wrestling. I let him go and he sank back to his task with a contented sigh.

Warwick had more stamina than me and as I didn't want to lose my load down Steven's throat, I suggested we swap positions. Being on the receiving end of blow jobs is my least favorite role. When it comes to oral sex, I've always believed it is more blessed to give than to receive.

On the other hand, Warwick believes that anything wrapped around his rampant prick – hand, mouth, ass, blow-up doll – is fine by him and he'll reward them with a juicy load. It may have something to do with the fact he's horny as fuck and ready for seconds within five or ten minutes of his initial ejaculation. He can come up to five times in a night if he's really horny and three times in a matter of hours if he's saved himself. Twice if he hasn't, although his cock stays hard regardless.

Warwick was already throat fucking our visitor before I'd even sheathed up in preparation for a session of ass pumping and dumping.

"We gonna go for it?" Warwick asked. "I don't think I can hold off much longer if he's gonna keep sucking like a Dyson."

Steven shook his head enthusiastically. I rammed his ass so hard he was impaled down to his Adam's apple on Warwick's cock, gagging enough that mucous leaked out his nose and the corners of his mouth, and his eyes watered.

"Holy Jesus," Warwick gasped. "I think my cock reached his navel that time."

I wasn't about to tell Warwick he was big, but not that big. Besides, Steven was doing things with his ass muscles that threatened my sanity. I was having a hard time keeping his hand away from his own cock because he obviously wanted to jerk himself off as we shot our loads, but I had other plans for him.

As I withdrew my cock until only the head remained inside him before plunging back in to my balls, I realized it would be only a short time before Steven would want two cocks at the same time up his rapacious ass. His boyfriend would be in for a hell of a ride to keep this one happy.

I saw Warwick pulling those faces he makes when he's trying with all his might to stop his money shot so I sped up my rhythm, fucking at different angles to find the tightest squeeze, while kissing my lover to show how much I appreciated his non-possessive nature. Steven squeezed his sphincter as I tore into his hole, humming his approval of what we were doing to his body.

With a roar, Warwick shot his creamy bolt into Steven's mouth and I followed seconds later blowing my cock snot deep inside our middle man's asshole. Steven was still incredibly frustrated because he hadn't come but I intended remedying that situation with all speed.

If I judged correctly, Steven was totally Warwick's type for extra-marital fucking and opportunities with such a gorgeous twink were few and far between so he wasn't going to waste any opportunity to indulge.

"You okay to go again?" I whispered.

"Hell, yeah," he mouthed.

He pulled his sticky cock out of Steven's insatiable craw as I handed him a condom which he slid on with expert ease. He shuffled off the coffee table as I withdrew from Steven's wet, warm ass to dispose of my mucky rubber. Warwick and I had partner share down to a fine art so he knew I was eager to get someone hard in my own ass. He maneuvered Steven so that I could lie on the carpet, raising my legs so my butt was within striking distance of his frustrated cock. It twitched in anticipation.

"Shit, you gonna let me fuck you?" Steven asked, incredulity in every word. "My boyfriend never bottoms."

"Be my guest," I panted, breaking open the foil, expertly rolling the protection down his cock praying that he wasn't so close he would spew before he got inside me. Warwick helped guide him toward the puckered prize after I'd applied lube to my butt. Steven slipped inside with minimal pain to me even though there was no finesse to his technique. He was obviously inexperienced in this regard.

Once I'd relaxed, I reached around his body to hold Steven's butt cheeks apart, giving Warwick ample opportunity to sink a hole in one. The weight of two men atop me pushed me along the carpet, giving me burn on my shoulder blades. I'd worry about that tomorrow because right now I was in cock heaven. I just wished there was another one or two guys to fill a few vacant mouths although that would have stopped the murmur of satisfaction all three of us hummed.

"You guys are amazing," Steven said. "I wish I had a relationship like this."

"Give it time," I said. "It doesn't happen overnight. Your boyfriend needs to feel secure before you can broach the subject."

To get me to shut up, Warwick fucked Steven hard which pushed my head against the leg of the coffee table. There's nothing more off-putting to a threesome that psychological counseling while in the throes of fucking.

What Steven lacked in experience he made up for in stamina, fucking my pliant asshole for a good fifteen minutes while Warwick 'unghed' his concentration to match him. The friction of Steven's stomach rubbing against my prick was making me sticky with pre-cum. They could keep fucking all night for all I cared but I was going to lose it very soon. I attempted to pant a warning but Warwick's action pushed Steven against my painful hard-on causing me to lose control, squirting spunk between our bodies. It set off a chain reaction, my ass muscles spasming around Steven's cock so that with a scream of "Oh fuck, I'm coming," he blew a load inside me while his sphincter gripped Warwick, milking a second load out of him.

Hot and sweaty, sticky with spooge, we collapsed side by side on the floor. It was quite a while before any of us spoke or even moved. We came around slowly, disposing of the rubbers, stretching cramped muscles, grinning like fools.

"Is it always that good?" Steven asked.

"I could tell you some horror stories," I said, remembering a few of the tragic cases we'd invited to share over the years.

"Don't scare him off," Warwick said, slapping my ass, before grabbing Steven's hand to help him off the floor. "Come on, time for a shower. You don't want to go back to your boyfriend smelling of some stranger's cum."

I knew what he was up to. There would be a repeat performance in the bathroom but this time it would be a duet. I was buggered.

Reading tarot really takes it out of me.

A Cook's Tour

"Pizza is the pampas grass of international cuisine. From the slopes of Mongolia to the outback of Australia, pizza has colonized the dining tables of the world." Jean-Pierre Gonflé, obviously middle-aged, arguably attractive, definitely pompous, most certainly opinionated, universally acclaimed as the latest cuisine guru, knew he had their attention. His success was not surprising. He was a superb cook, a delightful raconteur, and a showman of the highest skill.

"So, if any of you here think you're going to pick up tips on the latest boutique pizza topping or the secrets to making your spaghetti more al dente then, I suggest, you are in the wrong place and should depart immediately back to your modest little kitchens in your modest little suburbs and continue to prepare your modest little meals for your modest little families and their modest little taste buds!"

There was some embarrassed coughing, an uncomfortable shifting in some seats, and a none-too-ironic smile from me as I surveyed the jerry-built kitchen in which über-chef Gonflé was about to cook a few basic dishes from his best-selling glossy tome, *The New Mediterranean Cuisine*. In it, he not only brings the minority cuisines of Malta, Crete, Sardinia, Albania, Libya, and Tunisia out of the closet, he drags them center stage. Center stage in this case being the local bookstore tucked away upstairs in one of the few modern semi-high rise shopping malls in Valletta's main pedestrian thoroughfare, Triq il-Repubblika, rather than the controlled, vastly superior environment of his cable television soundstage, from which he usually beamed each weekday afternoon.

My interest was purely nationalistic. My parents had migrated from Malta to Australia when I was five. I still had fond memories of home-cooked aljotta, stuffat tal-fenek, bragoli, brungiel mimli, pudina tal-ħobż, and the delicious Lenten almond cake, kwarezimal. My visit to the place of my birth coincided with one of Gonflé's periodic world jaunts to pick up new cuisine ideas or, more usually, to promote a new glossy book that people would queue up to buy for the startlingly tactile photographs. I had flicked through the pages to ensure the inclusion of the nostalgic dishes before I had coughed up the rather steep purchase price, but the photographs, thanks to modern digital technology, were so lifelike the bouquet of my mother's kitchen, her private domain in a house over-run with men and boys, seemed to imbue the pages as lovingly as they did my memory.

I arrived early to have Gonflé personalize my book, but he seemed preoccupied by the lack of public adoration to which he felt himself entitled. My enquiry as to what dishes he would be preparing that afternoon was met with the gruff response that unless the crowds materialized very shortly, not only would there be no cooking demonstration of any kind, but there would be no Gonflé either.

The bookstore owner cringed at the hissed jibes, probably wondering how he could have over-estimated the popularity of his insufferable guest. But the renowned chef reserved his most venomous frustration for his obviously long-suffering assistant. I first spied the lad, in his early twenties, hovering on the outskirts of his master's benevolence, ensuring the books were stacked so that Gonflé's back cover portrait was prominently displayed, and harassing customers into the shop. Eventually, to the relief of all, the crowds appeared as surely as Gonflé's good humor.

But now he was bored. The audience clamored for cooking hints, the answers to which were all contained in his overpriced volume. He was trapped by the inanity of the questions, his reputation for sparkling, sarcastic wit, and his provocative pronouncements on everything from global warming to salmon farms versus wild salmon, bogged down in the minutiae of the common or garden western kitchen.

I waited for a break in the perfunctory responses before jumping in with a provocative question about culinary obesity being the pornography of the twenty-first century. I knew it was a subject close to his heart, and I had fed him an opportunity to pontificate at leisure. His assistant glanced my way. I smiled my best cocksucker smile after feeding Jean-Pierre the lines that would allow him to shine, and shine he did for the remainder of the session. The audience rose as one after his twenty-minute tour de force, going away marveling that his skills as a raconteur equaled his culinary skills.

His assistant came over as I dawdled to leave.

"Excuse me," he said. "But Chef Gonflé would like to thank you personally for your perceptive question, if you have a moment to spare."

I told him I would be only too glad and made my way over to where a gaggle of fans were all attempting to outdo each other in their adulation. He glanced my way, looked heavenward sighing as if to say, "the price of fame, eh?' His assistant began to clear away the cooking items and, in a mood of generosity, I offered to help.

Jean-Pierre leaned over, whispering, "I would be most grateful if you could wait around."

I looked at my watch, told him that I was not required elsewhere for another hour or so, and that I would be more than happy to wait. He turned his attention back to his admirers, his smile frozen in place.

I introduced myself to the young man as I helped stack dishes and saucepans into a large box. "Luca."

"Michel," he replied. "Merci, I appreciate the help."

I smiled in sympathy. "The star gets all the groupies, the roadie gets all the shit."

"Oh, I'm not the roadie. I'm ..." He stopped and looked away.

The box was full.

"Where to?" I asked.

"The car park. Jean-Pierre's van is parked there. We have to use the tradesman's elevator." There was a decided distaste to his voice.

Michel led me through a number of cinder block corridors until we came to the old goods elevator. Because he had insisted on taking the heavier load, I pressed the button for him. The elevator grumbled to our floor, where its doors wheezed open. It was crowded with trolleys as well as battered cardboard boxes from some half unloaded delivery. We barely had room to move. Michel was forced back against the boxes still holding his precious cargo. As we passed the fifth floor, I slammed my fist into the stop button.

"What are you doing?" he asked.

I moved in closer, my breath on his neck, my hands fumbling at his trousers. I pulled down the zip to plunge my hand inside under the waistband of his jockeys. He panicked at my presumption.

"It's okay," I said. "Your cock wants it even if you don't."

It was the truth because his cock sprang to life at my touch. I pulled his foreskin down; he shuddered as I rubbed my thumb across the tip. It came away sticky.

"Oh, for God's sake, don't," he moaned. "I'll come."

Speed was necessary, as I knew the elevator was in constant use. I squatted uncomfortably, face to face with his cock. I undid his belt, pulling his trousers down so I could get closer to the musky balls, licking them while inserting my finger in his ass as I wrapped my lips around his cock. I slid gently along the length of his smooth twink cock, my tongue lapping the underside and flicking his knob as his prick pulled back.

"Oh, God," he moaned out again.

The elevator juddered, moving again.

Michel's 'Oh, Gods' took on an air of panic. I pushed my face ever faster into his pubic hair, swallowing his cock to its root. He felt me gag, the constriction around his cock bringing him to the edge. I thought he would drop the dishes on me as I sucked faster and faster as the elevator jolted downwards. Then I felt his sphincter tighten around my finger as he squirted deep into my mouth. I licked my lips, stood up after carefully pushing his cock back into his underpants and zipping him up, so that we were the picture of perfect propriety as the doors opened to the car park.

The building manager looked puzzled at Michel's flushed face.

"Everything okay?" he asked.

"Perfect," I replied.

He almost dropped his other bundle as he stepped from the elevator; his legs had turned to rubber. I caught him and the box of dishes in time. At the van, he unlocked the back door to reveal a mobile kitchen stocked with just about everything Jean-Pierre would ever need, all packed away neatly. Michel squatted inside, slid the case of culinary items into their designated slot as easily as I hoped to slide my cock into his ass, now that there was room for me. Clambering on board, I pushed him back, slamming the door behind me.

"Jean-Pierre will be expecting us," he said, his eyes widening in surprise.

Ripping down his trousers, I turned him over, exposing his perfect round ass covered in wisps of blond hair. I had to squat in the cramped confines to kiss his little puckered asshole while fumbling with my own jeans, my cock screaming for release. I had them around my knees as my finger found his steamy hole. This was not going to be an easy spit job. I looked around. Well, if it was good enough for Marlon Brando, it was good enough for me. I smeared the butter over his asshole, probing the grease inside. He shuddered as my finger entered him deeply, just giving him time to get used to it before I pushed my cock against his sphincter.

He gasped in pain at first. I stopped until he got used to it then he pushed back against me until I slid inside, his asshole as fiery as paprika. "It won't take me long," I said. I was aching to possess him even if only for a night. Failing that, a fuck in his boyfriend's van would have to do.

Did I feel guilty about cuckolding the world famous chef? No, not really. This kid was born to be fucked, and if Jean-Pierre was such a greedy bastard as to keep it to himself then…

I ground my teeth in concentration and thrust so hard I almost knocked Michel over. He took this as the advance notice of my approaching orgasm by bracing himself, ramming his asshole back along my cock, squeezing. I groaned. The tension in my balls squirted string after string of cum into his ass until I collapsed on his back.

"That was fucking great," he whispered, "but I have to get back."

Well, what was I expecting? A honeymoon?

He moved forward until my cock popped out of his ass. He wiped the butter and cum with a cloth serviette from one of the world's classiest restaurants, then passed it to me. After wiping myself clean, I pocketed it. In no time at all we were back in the bookshop where Jean-Pierre gave us both a puzzled once over before the last of the stragglers, realizing they were going to get no further with the chef, bade farewell.

Finally, Jean-Pierre turned the full force of his personality to me. It was difficult not to like the man.

"I do so appreciate you taking the time to help Michel," he said without a hint of irony. "But particularly for your perspicacious questions."

I mumbled as modestly as I could to suggest it was the least I could do for greatness such as his.

"We know no one in this godforsaken hole." He offered a half-shrug. "Please excuse me for insulting your home town," he said with the sincerity of a bored preacher.

"Insult away," I encouraged. "You're a man of the world, much too sophisticated for a small city like this one. But we are grateful, nonetheless, that you should visit us."

"I was wondering if, perhaps, it is not too short a notice and would not inconvenience you, if you would care to join us for dinner at our hotel tonight." He smiled. "Not the hotel restaurant, mind you, superb as it is," he added quickly. "But I always insist on a hotel suite with a kitchen."

"It would be an honor to sup with Jean-Pierre Gonflé at his own table." I was soaping him up in an attempt to get to Michel again, but I did not see how I was going to manage it.

He wrote the hotel name plus a time on one of his ostentatiously embossed cards; assured me that there was no need to bring anything at all apart from my good self and my, uh, good wife, but seemed well pleased when I told him I was single. He smiled again. "A good-looking man like yourself, single? Quel domage."

They were staying, naturally enough, in the finest suite in the finest serviced apartments, courtesy of his publisher, in the Portomaso complex, a hotel, residential and marina development on the site of the old Fort Spinola. I walked casually along the St. Julian's waterfront, radiantly peaceful but for the choking diesel fumes of the antiquated yellow buses, vehicles that in most other countries would have been retired years ago, with their shrines to various saints to protect the drivers from the narrow winding streets and notorious car traffic. Up past the bustling restaurants and pastizzi parlors of Spinola Bay, on to the hushed luxury that is Portomaso where expensive yachts, way beyond the buying power of the locals, bobbed ostentatiously in the marina.

When Michel answered the door to their suite, I gave him a delighted smile, a quick squeeze of his cock, and a hurried surreptitious kiss on the lips. He leaned into my ear, "No praise is too much. There is no such thing as an excess of lip smacking, loud chewing or appreciative gastronomic sound effects."

I handed him the bottles I had brought with me. He took them gingerly, a look of horror crossing his handsome young face. "I hope you haven't tried to impress," he whispered.

I grinned. "Uh huh."

He gave a disappointed sigh that signified all was already lost as he ushered me into the suite. In one corner of the combined living/dining area was a well-equipped kitchen in which Jean-Pierre was fussing. As Michel approached with the wrapped wine, I watched as a smile of triumph lit up Gonflé's face. It was time to play Let's Humiliate the Guest. Or so he believed. I smiled back—a smile just a little less bright, a little less superior than the über-chef's. I didn't wish to upstage him. Michel looked heartbroken as he handed the precious bottles over. He gazed at the floor not wishing to witness my humiliation. I liked the lad even more for his consideration. But he underestimated me.

Jean-Pierre ripped the paper from around the wine and, for a split second, his smile froze before he let out an almighty whoop of laughter that made Michel look up. In one hand, he held a bottle of Romanian Vampire Pinot Grigio, in the other a bottle of Vampire Cabernet Sauvignon. Michel winked at me. With my choice of wine, I had broken the ice. Jean-Pierre clapped me on the back.

"Most dinner guests attempt to impress Jean-Pierre with the most expensive, the most unavailable, the most desirable wines and spirits in the world." He had a habit of referring to himself in the third person. "But you, you have called his bluff. You see Jean-Pierre is particular about his food, his wine, but he is not pretentious." Again he laughed. "Romanian wines are good, solid tasting, much in demand," he started to lecture. "Pah, but who cares, it's in the tasting, is it not?"

I agreed. Michel was given the task of opening the bottle of cabernet sauvignon to allow it to breathe. Jean-Pierre led me to the sofa while Michel busied himself in the kitchen. The chef gazed absent-mindedly at his assistant. "Michel is everything to Jean-Pierre. Jean-Pierre will teach him everything he knows. He has a natural flare. In time he may even surpass the master. Jean-Pierre will hate that of course." He shrugged. "But that is the nature of the beast. He is quite magnificent, is he not?"

"Indeed," I responded truthfully.

"And did you fuck him gently or fuck him hard while you were in the car park?"

Michel stopped stock still in the kitchen.

"Perhaps it would be best to ask Michel, for as with wine, it's in the tasting."

Again Jean-Pierre laughed.

"And are you here to steal him from me?" he asked without rancor.

"I have nothing to offer him. At least not like you have."

"What about love?" He tried hard to keep the smirk out of his voice.

"I don't love Michel," I said. "But to answer your initial question, no, I did not come here with the intention of stealing Michel from you. Perhaps, if the occasion arose, to love him for a moment or an hour, but that's all."

The subject of our conversation smiled.

"You would be a formidable foe," Jean-Pierre admitted.

I bowed my head slightly at the tribute I had been paid because I knew it was a compliment of the highest order. The chef did nothing lightly. He called Michel over and, without making a show of his proprietorship, told Michel to look after me while he finished preparing the meal.

Michel's unfolded his background dispassionately, and like Jean-Pierre, he told it in the third person. In his case though, the early Michel of whom he spoke was a different person altogether to the young man before me. His life had changed when he'd approached Jean-Pierre in a nightclub to ask for money in exchange for favors.

"I declined his offer," Jean-Pierre said from the kitchen, reverting now to the first person because we were talking of intensely personal matters. "But told him I would cook him a meal and that he could stay the night. No strings attached."

Michel's features softened with nostalgia. "I accepted. And here I am."

"Hmm," I said. "I think there's some of the story missing here. Probably the X-rated section."

"No, no." Michel said quickly. "Jean-Pierre fed me the best meal I had ever tasted, and then allowed me to sleep in his bed. He slept on the sofa. As I was still there the next day, had stolen nothing, he cleared out a spare room, setting it up as a bedroom for me to use as I wished. He never once threatened or forced me into a relationship with him. In fact, I was so used to being ordered around that his lack of aggression confused me. I didn't know how to relate to someone who treated me as an equal, not a paid sexual companion. It was almost a year before I gave up the street life totally to become a permanent guest in the spare bedroom. He hired me as his assistant on his cooking show. Paid me handsomely. Still, he asked only that I do my job well, nothing more. It was a few months longer before I took my pillow to Jean-Pierre's bedroom. I never left."

"But," Jean-Pierre added, "Just as no one but the most obsessive would eat the same meal day after day, so it is with lovemaking. Variety adds sauce to the dish."

I understood.

"The first course is ready," Jean-Pierre announced with a flourish.

We huddled together like orphans at one end of a magnificent table that could seat ten, with Jean-Pierre in pride of place at the head, while Michel and I sat opposite each other. The entrée was dandelion petals, roots, and stems poached in oat milk.

The chef made much of the dish's origin and its preparation, closing his eyes in almost a parody of ecstasy as he savored it. In return, I ran my tongue along my lips after I had eaten the delicacy in a genuine show of delight, dabbing my mouth suggestively with the linen serviette, transferring to it the remnants of flavor and my appreciation.

The next course — I'd been warned there were to be five — was pearl meat tossed in a wok with shiitake mushrooms, a splash of soy sauce, and chopped fresh chives and ginger.

"Pearl meat is the flesh of the oyster that surrounds the pearl," Jean-Paul explained. "Only available for a brief period each year when they harvest the pearl oysters."

The third consisted of terrine of duck liver with cardamom sugar, apricot spiced with juniper and macadamia nuts served with cuttlefish ink.

I had never eaten a meal like this before. I am never likely to again. I could ill afford the world's best restaurants let alone my own private world-class chef. My enthusiasm for his culinary genius was effusive and sincere. Gonflé obviously appreciated my abject surrender to his skills, seeming to sport an erection each time he stood to go to the kitchen.

The last of the savory dishes was hake fillet with baby garlic, hazelnut praline, soured cream and purslane. The atmosphere in the room was heady and close aided immeasurably by copious quantities of wine. As we ate, I was again voluble in my appreciation. Jean-Pierre openly played with his cock beneath the table. I was having trouble concentrating on the food, superb as it was and, groping under the table, I discovered Michel, too, was hard in his jeans.

"Never be afraid to savor every morsel," Jean-Pierre purred. "Cuisine is such a transitory art. It can never be exactly recaptured, so it has to be savored now. It will never happen the same way again. I know you are a man of vigorous appetites," he said to me. "I think your appetites will lead you into adventures that the, shall we call them, more ordinary palates may find too experimental."

Michel cleared away the plates.

"My one concession this evening is to allow Michel to prepare the dessert," Gonflé said proudly.

"Rhubarb and woodruff with skyr and sweetbreads," Michel boasted.

"Good food is as satisfying as good sex, mon ami," Jean-Pierre smiled. "For some, it is better."

Michel brought the dishes to the table. "Taste," he ordered us.

It was exquisite. I burbled my appreciation as best I could. Jean-Pierre spooned it into his mouth and groaned exquisitely. My cock was as hard as the china plate. All pretense at refinement was gone. Gonflé was jerking his cock as he ate. Michel smiled an invitation. Now I knew why the chef had not troubled to consummate his relationship with Michel that first night or for months afterward. He preferred the erotic stimulation of gastronomy.

I circled the table quickly, pulled Michel to his feet, stripping his clothes from him as Jean-Pierre burbled his encouragement. Pushing him across the table, over the detritus of the meal, I hoisted Michel's legs over his head and lowered my mouth to his ass, licking, sniffing and chewing it as hungrily as any of the courses I had consumed that night. Michel's ass was equal to any of Gonflé's confections. My cock twitched in anticipation as I probed Michel's hole with my tongue, clumsily divesting myself of my clothes.

I took Michel in my arms, gently pushing against his asshole. I intended to make this last. If Gonflé meant his lover as an entrée, I was determined to make him a main course. My cock slid in smoothly. Michel took me easily down to my balls. I leaned in, kissed him gently, savoring the taste of his dessert lingering on both our tongues. I had never felt such passion, such rawness before.

I moved my hips firmly but not roughly, fucking him with as much love and attention as he had put into the preparation of his fare. Jean-Pierre was right; there is as much passion in cooking as there is in sex, but my cock had a different preference to my stomach. As the chef began to shout his encouragement, I sped up to meet his obscene demands. Michel clung to me, watching my face as I grimaced in an attempt to ward off orgasm. I wrapped my hands around his hard cock, jerking it lightly, making him gasp. He attempted to take my hand away, but I was too close, keeping up the rhythm while I fucked his welcoming asshole. As I increased speed, I pumped harder, with greater urgency.

As I blew my load inside him, I let out a bellow of appreciation, not just for the fine male ass in which I had my cock buried, but in appreciation of life, of food, all the finer things that made living so sweet. Michel exploded over my hand. Jean-Pierre, wide eyed in appreciation, anointed our sexual coupling with his sperm benediction.

Michel lay slumped across the table panting, while I attempted to gain my breath back. Gonflé had collapsed back into his chair. I was about to retract my cock when Michel pulled me closer to him. He sat up, kissing me without reserve. I was wary that now we had all cum everything would change. But Jean-Pierre showed no inclination we should stop our activity.

"Jean-Pierre is a middle-aged man," he said as he got up from the table, "And it is time for his bed. But you two have the stamina, the appetites of youth where quantity sometimes outweighs quality. I'll bid you bon soir."

I thanked Jean-Pierre for his hospitality, even more for his generosity. He informed me that breakfast would be at 8am—on the dot. It was obvious I would be spending the night, spending the night with Michel in the second bedroom.

Michel kissed Jean-Pierre good night before turning his attention to me. His tongue explored my mouth as if he were tasting a favorite dish. I envied the two of them, their loving relationship, their ability to incorporate new dishes, new tastes. I'm not sure that I would have been able to share Michel so generously with the outside world had he been mine.

His cock was hardening again, one of the delights of youth. Mine would take a little longer but harden again it would, particularly under Michel's persistent expert manipulation. But for the moment he had other ideas.

He held my butt cheeks in his hands then slowly pulled them apart so he could push a finger toward my hole. I sighed as he pressed gently. He increased the number of fingers until he felt he had loosened me enough. Then pushed me face down over the table and his cock tore into my ass.

I hoped there would be at least five courses to our lovemaking.

Topping the Pizza Delivery Boy

Billy gets really frisky around Christmas. It takes all my strength to keep him in check. He has the sort of personality that's prone to over-indulge in recreational substances and booze, particularly if forced on him by a second party, and that, in turn, leads to an abundant over-indulgence in Billy's favorite party-time recreation: sex. Billy can be, given the right circumstances, a slut.

It starts in September, the southern hemisphere spring. His libido is lethargic during the winter, he almost hibernates but as soon as the sun goes from watery warmth to slightly sizzling it's off with the shirts and the jumpers and on with the T-shirts, singlets and very tight shorts. He is continually horny, like he comes on heat. You can set your seasonal clock to his sexual behavior. Most of the time he keeps it in check, merely exhibiting himself and his availability. Fortunately, I've got what it takes between my legs although it's a roller coaster ride trying to keep up.

It doesn't happen often but when he does break out, courtesy of the aforementioned libido enhancing drugs or booze, or some perceived slight from me – let's face it, just about anything sets him off when he gets that 'itch' – it takes all my strength of character and my trampled pride to indulge him, rescue him, and take him back home. I love the silly bugger, that's my only excuse.

This particular Christmas was going to be a lousy one. We were pretty broke, not an uncommon occurrence, the mortgage was getting behind, I was worried sick, and Billy's part-time kitchen work was drying up when we least expected it. Firms were economizing on Christmas parties. I was working as much overtime as possible so I was getting home too buggered to bugger Billy who was becoming friskier by the day. I knew the signs, but I also knew that a perfunctory fuck would not satisfy him any more than the rubber dildos he used regularly on his own ass when I was not home.

He's not totally insensitive and realized my worry over apartment repayments as well as ongoing expenses was playing havoc with my sexual appetite and my ability to please him. But I didn't want to burden him with things beyond his control. For his peace of mind I kept most of the bad news from him, sharing only the good. There was blessed little of that at the time. I decided we'd sit down and have 'the talk' about finances in the New Year, and the very real option of selling up and downsizing. Let him enjoy the holiday period.

Meanwhile, I just had to endure his constant harping on my lack of sexual enthusiasm, my reluctance to go out partying, my near permanent total exhaustion, and my lack of interest in anything at all he was interested in. After another of his particularly self-indulgent and whiny attacks on my worth as a lover, I'm afraid I'd had about as much as I could stand. Okay, so it was my fault for not taking him into my confidence, and I would probably do things differently given my life over again and knowing what I know now, but he pushed me too far. He knew how to press my buttons. He screamed at me after I'd turned him down again about going to a show that would cost two days' pay. "You're no fuckin' fun at all anymore. Maybe I should have stayed with Jerry."

The silence that followed was deafening. Jerry, after all, was my former butt ugly boss, who had not only had his way with Billy in front of me once, but had also managed to steal Billy away from me for a number of months until he got tired of him and passed him on to another couple who seriously abused his trust. As a result, Billy had a tattoo which read 100% Pure Slut on his butt. It was only with a great deal of public humiliation, patience, and ingenuity that I managed to win him back. Now he was throwing it in my face.

He must have known he'd gone too far, his look of regret said as much, but he was damned if he would apologize. It was not in his nature. And it was not in my nature to hit him, or walk away and slam the door. No, I had to be sarcastic.

I went to the bureau drawer and scribbled a phone number on a Post-It! note and handed it to him. "Here. That's the last known phone number for your pal Jerry. If he's not there, I'm sure they'll pass on a message. Maybe he can pay you again so we can get out of this hideous financial mess we're in. The apartment's in the balance."

Then I walked off and slammed the door. Only later, I thought perhaps I could have phrased it better.

Normally when we have a quarrel, one or the other of us climbs into bed and apologizes with a kiss and a cuddle rather than let the argument stew. Not that night. Billy slept in the spare bedroom. And the next night. And from then on. We were civil to each other but we ate our meals separately. Billy kept out of my way when I was getting ready for work and when I came home late at night exhausted.

Our blowup spurred him on to seek a job – any job. I found pages of the local job market classifieds circled but he obviously had had little luck as they also had a large cross through them. He was always in bed, in the guest room, every morning when I left for work. I would tiptoe in, arrange the sheet and blanket around him, and peck him lightly on the forehead or the cheek, before leaving quietly.

As September rolled into October, the unexpected occurred. One night I came back from work and Billy was ironing a waistcoat in the living room while watching television. He looked like his old self again, and the smell of warm food wafted from the kitchen. He welcomed me home by flinging his arms around me and giving me a wet, sloppy kiss and a quick grope. He sat me down and served me dinner, playing the attentive lover, to the extent he gave me a tasty blow job as I sat watching TV to unwind. I should have known he was buttering me up.

He was so eager with his news, he jumped to his feet while he was still swallowing the load I'd dumped in his mouth, wiped his lips with the back of his hand, and danced about the room. "I've got a job! I've got a job!"

"That's wonderful news," I cheered.

"It's only for a month or two in the lead-up to Christmas, but I'll be able to help with the phone bill and the power."

"You don't have to do that," I said, but secretly glad he would be bringing in a little extra cash. It all helped. "What sort of job is it?"

He suddenly looked embarrassed, like he'd oversold his prospects. "I get to wear a uniform. You stay right there and I'll show you."

I had no trouble following orders, I was too exhausted to move, especially after a Billy Oral Special. That was another of the problems I had with Billy when he became uncontrollable sexually. He had a reputation. No, not in the bad sense. Well, not in any way that I would consider bad. He was known to be one of the best fucks in the city. Especially if you got him in the right mood, and there were plenty of people out there who wanted to get him in the right mood because he was one of the cutest little blond fuckers you ever laid eyes on. And he worked out in the gym to keep his body as taut and terrific as any top model, although it was his ass that was his salient feature. Correction: as superb as his butt was, it was actually his asshole that was the source of his fame.

While he was changing into his new working clothes he chatted from the bedroom. "With my skills, or should I say my almost complete lack of, there wasn't much going so don't get disappointed and give me that lecture on holding out for something commensurate with my abilities. No one's hiring in that field." Billy was an unemployed sous chef. "Close your eyes. Go on, close them. Are they closed?"

"Yeah," I called.

I heard activity as Billy obviously got himself in position to pose.

"Open them. Ta da!" He threw his arms in the air as if he were a Broadway diva, although in the outfit he was wearing he looked more like a sleazy 42nd Street stripper before the neo-moralists moved in to clean up the area.

I had steeled myself against every contingency I could think of. Except the one that confronted me. I smiled weakly as I looked at Billy, practically naked, eagerly awaiting my approval. He twirled on the spot as if his uniform was something that would not be out of place on the Oscar's Red Carpet. It was more likely to get him arrested.

"Billy, I can practically see your asshole when you turn around."

"Yeah," he said patting his butt. "They said they'll get me a better fit once I start. They just loaned me this so I could get used to wearing it. And could get some practice in."

"What's to get used to?" I asked, a tinge of sarcasm creeping in. "You're wearing a bright orange cap, a waistcoat, a pair of the tightest vibrant orange shorts I've ever seen and which will strangle all the sperm in your balls if you don't get out of them soon, and a pair of orange sneakers."

"Tandoori," he said, with a touch of disappointment in his voice.

"What?"

"It's tandoori, not orange."

I had to salvage his pride. "I bet you'll be the sexiest pizza delivery boy in the country."

"You think?" he said, perking up a little.

"I didn't think they employed men for the job," I said.

"They don't. I'm the first. The only. It's a test run. The company is interested in tapping the gay market."

In that outfit the gay market would be mighty interested in tapping Billy.

Every fiber of my being wanted to scream, 'You'll take this job over my dead body,' but I had to be supportive. The distinctive orange, excuse me, tandoori outfit was normally the domain of a voluptuous female, usually just over the right side of the age of consent, and who didn't mind showing off as much of her body in public as legally permissible while flirting outrageously with male customers. It was rumored, some of the girls, particularly college students, were not averse to allowing a little feel of their perky tits, sometimes allowing further liberties if the tip was large enough. It was all hearsay. What wasn't in doubt is that Pizza with Everything was run by Billy's uncle, Ram, his nickname supposedly because of what he had hanging between his legs. He was the black sheep of Billy's family. He'd married a former porn star, twenty years his junior, and made no secret of his prodigious appetite, not only for pizza, but for the nubile young women who worked for him.

"What exactly do you have to do in this job?" I asked casually.

"Hey, don't worry, love." Billy came and sat on my knee to give me a reassuring cuddle. "It's nothing like that. I may flirt a little to get a bigger tip but I won't be delivering anything that isn't on the menu."

Billy finds it almost impossible to lie. He gives himself away when he's guilty but I didn't notice any tell-tale signs as he explained his job. Still, he may not intend straying from the menu but there would be some guys out there who would be trying everything to ensure he did. Hell, he didn't need a job as a pizza delivery boy to come across those temptations.

"When do you start?" I asked, giving his new job my imprimatur.

Billy showered me with kisses. "Tomorrow. The only bugger is that I'll be at work when you get home at night. The job starts at 5pm until last orders. We won't get to see a lot of each other over the next few weeks but it will make Christmas better, won't it, Steve?"

Billy was so eager for validation I made all the right noises. When he got tired of prancing around in his ultra-revealing outfit, he led me to the bedroom and I leisurely put his marble-hard butt and its warm inviting hole to good use, reminding myself that I was the incredibly lucky boyfriend of the hottest ass in the country.

When we were lying arm in arm after we'd both dumped a load, I nuzzled Billy's neck and gave him the good news. "With you earning an income we can afford to have our usual Christmas party," I announced triumphantly.

I expected squeals of delight but all I got was silence.

"I thought you'd be pleased," I said.

"What's say we skip the party and put the money toward paying bills?"

Something was up, apart from my good self, because Billy had never been practical with money before.

"I thought our Christmas party was the highlight of the year." I was slightly miffed at his seeming display of ingratitude.

"Uh, no, not really," he mumbled.

"What do you mean, not really?"

"Here we go," he sighed. "I was hoping to avoid this argument."

"There won't be an argument," I lied. "I just want to know why you've suddenly turned against the party."

"It's not the party as such." He was choosing his words carefully. "It's the people who come to them."

"They're all our closest friends," I said.

"Your closest friends."

"My friends are your friends."

"Nah, your friends are sleazy scumbags who are all trying to fuck me behind your back and trying to get me to move in with them." I saw him tense, waiting for the verbal onslaught.

The idea was so ludicrous, I laughed.

"I know you're hot, Billy. And your reputation is all over the state, but my friends wouldn't do that."

He shrugged like he didn't want to argue the point. "Okay, have it your way. But there is maybe one or two of your closest mates who haven't seriously tried it on with me when you're not looking or you're not home and who haven't offered me money, an overseas holiday, whatever I want, to move in with them."

"I bet you wouldn't say that again to their face."

"I bet I would," he said and rolled over in the bed.

"If it's true, and I say 'if', why haven't you told me before?"

"I didn't want to upset you."

I snapped. I couldn't help myself. "Well, if you didn't dress like a slut and give everyone the 'come on, fuck me' routine—"

He smiled sweetly. "I thought you liked to watch me make a slut of myself. I thought it turned you on."

"The problem with you, Billy, is you have no self-control. You have no discernment when it comes to who you flirt with. Even worse, who you...play with."

"I thought that's what being a slut was all about."

"Not with my friends!"

"They're not friends. I've tried to tell you for years. They're sleazebags who hang around you in the hope of sinking their cocks into me."

We were back to where we started.

He got out of bed, grabbing his pillow. "I think it best if I sleep in the spare bedroom permanently." Our rapprochement had been short-lived.

I could not bring myself to ask him to stay. I'd upset him, not least by calling him a slut, the term of abuse that others used when they were trying to humiliate him. I lay awake for hours mulling over what he'd said. I couldn't bear to believe that most of my friends and, yes, I had to agree they were my friends, not his, would behave so crassly toward him. I fell asleep wondering.

The next week was painful. We barely spoke to each other. His excuse was that he didn't want to disturb me when he came in late and didn't want me to disturb his sleep when I got up in the morning. But I'd lie awake until all hours waiting for his familiar sounds and smells before I could fall asleep. Only once did I try to cajole him back into our bedroom. I'd kissed him and tasted the spice of another man's spunk on his lips and tongue and had recoiled. That put paid to our reconciliation. My look of shock must have registered more disapproval than I had felt. Billy's exile continued: my torment made a thousand times worse by my imagination.

My work was suffering, I couldn't sleep, and I was an accident waiting to happen. I had to get help. I decided to seek the advice of two of my closest friends, Murray and Dale. They'd had similar ups and downs in their long-term relationship, and I'd helped them through those times, mainly by the example of Billy's and my rock solid commitment.

I drove over to their place one night after Billy had left for work. He would detest that I'd brought other people into our problems, but I had nowhere else to turn as Billy would not talk to me, always pleading that he was 'too exhausted.' Dale made me a stiff drink when he saw how upset I was. "We were about to eat, do you want to join us?" he asked.

"If I'm not intruding."

"After all you've done for us, it would be a pleasure," Murray said.

"Trouble at home?" I did not like the snarky tone to Dale's voice. Billy's accusations were poisoning me and made me suspicious of everyone and their motives.

"That's what I came to talk about."

Murray put his arm around my shoulder in comfort as Dale handed me my bourbon and ice. I gulped the first mouthful, requiring the courage of alcohol to confess that my perfect relationship was anything but. Dale refilled my glass to better lubricate my tongue. I was about to launch into my tale of woe, when there was a knock at the door.

"That'll be the pizza," Murray said smiling.

"That will cheer you up," Dale said.

"Nothing like a bit of eye candy with your hot meal." Murray was positively slobbering.

"You invited me to stay for pizza?"

"It's pizza night, we have pizza every Wednesday night."

I begged off joining them. "I think I'd better go."

"Stay a minute." Murray was trying to be supportive but he was making things much more difficult. "Steve, this guy is supposed to be amazing. Delivers the pizza and does anything at all you want and more. He's supposed to be the hottest thing on two legs. Everyone we know says he's worth every cent, though the pizzas don't come cheap."

There was no reason to believe it was Billy at the door but my head told me otherwise. Murray and Dale obviously had no idea as to the identity of the pizza delivery boy or else were consummate actors. I knew they weren't after attending their diabolically bad performances in an amateur all-male production of *The Women* the year before.

"Is there another way out?"

"Not unless you climb out the window," Dale said.

"I'm begging you. As a friend. Don't tell him I'm here."

"Don't tell who?" Murray seemed genuinely baffled.

"The pizza boy."

"Why? Are you having it off with him? Are you on a low carb diet and you're scared he might tell..."

The look of horror on my face must have given the game away.

"Oh. My. God." Dale could scarcely conceal the glee in his voice.

Murray was less obvious. "The pizza delivery boy is Billy?"

"Did you order from Pizza with Everything?"

Murray nodded his head.

My heart sank. "It could be Billy. Please don't tell him I'm here. He'll think I'm checking up on him."

"Why would he think that? We're friends after all." I couldn't detect any sarcasm in Murray's question.

"He's been rather secretive about his job lately and that's caused a bit of friction." I thought that half-truth would satisfy them.

Murray was all sympathy. "You think he's delivering a bit more than pizza?"

My face said it all.

"We heard this pizza boy puts out," Dale said.

"Not that we were interested in that. But his ass is supposed to be something special. And Dale was getting a little jealous every time someone mentioned it."

"So it's not likely to be Billy," Dale was vicious when he got started.

The knock was more insistent this time.

I pleaded. "Please don't tell him."

Murray's reply was less than convincing. "Uh, okay."

Dale crossed his heart but looked rather smug about it.

"Just in there," Murray said, pointing to the walk-in closet near the door. "You'll be able to see and hear everything without being seen yourself."

"When he's gone I think you'd better come out and tell us the whole story," Murray said.

I ducked into the coat closet near the front door which had a ventilation hole at eye height and a great view of the living area.

Dale opened the door and snickered. "Hey, Billy. How are you, mate? Come in."

He draped his arm over Billy's shoulder in a much-too-familiar manner considering he purported not to like him. Or was he doing this for my benefit? Surely Billy would deliver the pizza, collect his money and go. He only ever expressed intense dislike of these too.

"Hey, Billy," Murray called. "Since when you been delivering pizza?"

"A few weeks now."

"You like the job?"

"Love it. I meet such interesting people."

"Pay good?" Dale asked. He'd always been mercenary.

"Oh, it's okay. I can make up for it with tips though."

Murray kept drawing him out. "Looking hot in that outfit, Billy. It doesn't leave much to the imagination."

"That's the whole point, I guess. The customers seem to like it."

"You must get hit on a lot."

Billy smiled. "Yeah."

"You know how to handle yourself if the buyers get too rough?"

Murray was a good mate. He was asking all the right questions. All the things he knew I couldn't ask without Billy thinking I was checking up on him.

"No one ever gets too rough for me." Billy never knew when to stop. I knew he was only being friendly because the job dictated it but there was a limit to revealing confidences.

"Let me see, you ordered the Spicy with Double Topping?"

"That's it."

"Uh," Billy hesitated. "You guys still want to go ahead now you know it's me?"

"Why wouldn't we?"

"I thought you guys didn't like me."

"We don't have to like you to do this," Dale said, running his hand over Billy's tight ass. "Aw, shit, Murray, feel this."

Murray squeezed Billy's butt and moaned his satisfaction.

"You up for it?" Murray asked.

"Sure," he smiled.

"Even though it's us?"

"That makes it even better," Billy said and pulled his vest open to reveal his six-pack and his rock hard pecs.

"I've fancied you guys ever since we were introduced."

"Fuck," Dale panted. "We've wanted to fuck your hot ass since forever, but Steve's so jealous he wouldn't let us near you."

"Think how fuckin' hot it will be now then."

"Will you tell him?" Dale asked.

"Fuck, no! Will you?"

"So he doesn't know you're doing this?" Murray was suspicious, and glanced toward where I was hiding. "This is not some sort of set-up?"

"No way. He knows I deliver pizza. That's all."

"What if he did know?" Murray was conflicted between me, his best friend watching the activity from my hiding place, and Dale's all-out assault on Billy that was happening in front of him, obviously uncaring about my feelings.

"Fuck him," Billy said. "It's my body."

"Cool," Dale said stripping Billy's shorts off. "Bend over, slut."

Billy, naked and already hard, bent over and grabbed his ankles. Dale kneeled and parted his cheeks, fingering his asshole. "He's all yours Murray." They were probably eager to begin in case I tried to put a stop to the activity.

I wasn't going to do that. Not yet, at any rate. I wanted to see how far my erstwhile friends would go. And I wanted to see just what sort of pizza delivery boy Billy really was. It looked as if he was every gay man's wet dream come true.

Dale had stripped off his clothes, his leaking cock looking mean and spiteful. With a scream of "Suck it, mongrel cunt whore," Dale slammed it into Billy's mouth choking him. Murray watched in awe as his boyfriend attacked mine. Billy opened his throat and Dale just slammed in and out until his cock was covered in puke and drool, the sounds of deep penetration gagging echoing around the living room. The ramrod face fuck kept up for a good five minutes until Dale relaxed and let Billy catch his breath.

"Fuck, Dale. I've never had my throat pounded so good. You like feeding it to me, huh? Watching it slide down my throat. Go on; choke me on your big hot cock.

Steve never feeds me enough cock, that's why I gotta get it outside."

Murray was still watching the action, playing with his own prick that seemed eager to get at Billy's ass. He must have been nervous because he kept glancing my way. The decision was taken out of his hands when Billy backed up, grabbed his cock, guiding it into his hole.

"What about Steve? I'm his best friend" Murray squeaked.

Billy sighed as he impaled himself right down to Murray's balls. "Don't give me that shit. You don't like Steve."

"Nah, never did like the fucker!" Dale agreed, watching his lover penetrate deep into Billy's butthole.

"Steve won't let me fuck his friends."

"Why not?" Dale asked.

"Too scared they'll be better than him, I guess."

"And are we better than him, Billy?" Dale asked.

"Fuck, yeah, do you even have to ask?" Billy grunted as Murray picked up the pace.

"You are so fuckin' nasty, Billy," Dale sat in an armchair watching the action and, behind that, my hiding spot. He was slowly jerking his cock with the remnants of Billy's puke. He was letting Billy run off at the mouth because he knew every word was a stab straight to my guts. "How many guys you had so far tonight?"

"Eight. You guys are the last order."

"Fuck, you're still so tight," Murray said. "Your ass in unbelievable."

"They don't all want to fuck me. Some want to watch me strip or suck me off. Some want me to be really nasty." He left the idea hanging.

"Are you a nasty whore, Billy?" Dale probed.

"You bet I am."

"A filthy cum-sucking slut?"

"That's me."

Nothing Dale said phased Billy. I hoped he wasn't leading him into a trap.

Murray was gasping. "Fuck, oh fuck. This is the best ass I have ever screwed! No wonder Steve doesn't want to share you."

Billy encouraged him. "Come on, Murray. Slam your cock into me. I want that hot hard cock of yours squirting spunk deep inside me. Then I'll lick you clean. That's it Murray, your cock feels so fuckin' good."

His voice was low and hypnotic and Murray was close. Billy got that look on his face when he's concentrating all his energy on his butthole, squeezing it like a suction cup around the invading prick.

Murray let out a strangulated scream. "Holy mother of god. I can't take any more." He humped against Billy's butt five or six times and collapsed on his back. He caught his breath and pulled free, spunk dribbling down Billy's leg, before pushing the slimy cock in Billy's mouth for a spit clean and polish. Then, still breathing heavily, he swapped places with Dale and sank exhausted into the chair.

Dale lay Billy on the rug and pushed his legs over his shoulders. Then, without any preliminaries, sank his cock right into Billy's guts, the previous spunk deposited there acting as lube. Dale wrapped his hand around Billy's throat, choking his head in position so they had to look each other in the eye. I could see Billy grit his teeth as he stared into the black eyes of his defiler. "Do your worst fucker," he hissed.

Ramming his cock into Billy, Dale rotated his hips to enter from a different angle each time, varying his thrusts to keep the man speared by his prick on the alert. Billy groaned which meant the fucker was getting to him. Dale was a magnificent animal and it was almost a pleasure to watch him plowing my far from defenseless boyfriend. I was hard. I undid my fly and dragged out my cock to gently apply pressure to the already leaking piss slit.

"Who's the best you've had tonight, Billy?"

"Fuck, no contest. You two. You both make me so fuckin' horny. I need your cocks inside me. I've needed them since that first time I met you. I wanted you to throw me down and fuck me right there and then."

"You're not just saying that, Billy?" Dale was no dummy.

"Fuck, no. I mean it. You guys are the hottest fuckers I ever met. Your cocks are just perfect for my cunt holes. You notice that way my ass muscle gripped when you were fucking me?" Both men agreed they had. "That was special just for you guys. It drives Steve wild. I promised him he would be the only guy I ever did it to."

"Shit, eh," Murray laughed.

Dale goaded. "What else will you do Billy that Steve wouldn't want you to?"

"Anything. Especially if it's real nasty."

Dale picked up pace, his body slapping loudly against Billy's butt. "You. Are. My. Kind. Of. Slut. Boy." Dale was obviously dumping a load inside my lover.

He pulled out and Billy slumped on the carpet, his ass in my direct line of sight.

Dale pulled him up on his knees, doggy style. "Show us your ass, Billy. Let's see the spunk we blew up that cum dump ass of yours."

Billy reached back to spread his cheeks, and cum dribbled out of his butt hole. Dale held a glass that he'd picked up from the kitchen, under the puffy ass lips. "Here, Billy. Push out the loads inside you."

Billy squeezed his ass, wads of cum drooling into the glass.

"How many loads, Billy?"

"Five. Plus your two."

"Fuckin' nasty!"

"Anything for you guys."

"Would you tell that to Steve if he was here now," Murray asked.

"Fuck, yeah."

"What would you tell him, Billy?" Dale asked.

"You guys know how to treat a cum dump slut."

Dale grabbed him hard again by the throat. "Say it louder, Billy!"

"Steve fucks like a girl," Billy shouted. "I need man cock like you guys."

"And you're not lying, Billy?"

"I'll show you how much I mean it. I'll stay for another session with you two off the clock, my treat. You can do whatever you want."

"What if we want to fuck you in front of Steve to teach him a lesson that he's got to share you?"

"I'd love that," Billy's mind was probably racing into the fantasy.

"What if we want our friends to fuck you?" Murray said.

"Bring them on."

Dale handed Billy the glass of slime. Billy raised it and said, "Skol. Here's to you guys, and loads more man cream." He tipped the glass and we watched fascinated as his throat muscles bobbed, swallowing the juice, gagging only once but keeping it down.

Dale was all admiration. "Fuck, that was hot."

Murray slapped Billy's face with his hard prick before sliding it between his lips, holding the back of his head obviously enjoying the warmth of Billy's slime-slicked throat. I watched Murray lean over, hooking his thumbs into Billy's sphincter, pulling it open.

"Fuck, that ass is so sweet, I bet everyone wants to fuck it," Murray said.

"You'd let them fuck it, too, wouldn't you, Billy?"

"Hell, yeah. I want to take every cock in the world."

"What's your hottest fantasy right now, Billy? If Steve was here to watch."

Billy groaned. "Shit, that's my dream. Get all Steve's friends who he thinks are so fuckin' cool, they all try to fuck me when he's not looking. Get them in one room."

"What then, Billy?"

"Get Steve over and make him watch every one of his so-called friends fuck my ass until I'm full of their spunk. Then make him suck it out, taste the slime they've been waiting to pump into me behind his back for years."

"Off the clock?"

"Yeah, I promised."

"Give us the names, Billy," Murray said.

"You guys are serious?" Billy asked.

"Deadly."

Billy looked like the cat that got the cream as he rattled off the names of my closest friends. Eight in all.

Mates who I thought were on my side. This would prove it one way or the other. One by one Dale dialed their numbers on Billy's mobile and invited them over to meet the famed pizza delivery boy that everyone was talking about. He didn't let on the delivery boy's identity. Two weren't home and one wanted to bring his boyfriend.

I should have put a stop to it, but I wanted to see who of my friends would stand up for me. Murray and Dale were counting on that to stop me from interrupting their game plan.

"Some of them should be here in about ten to fifteen minutes. Those that live further away could be up to half an hour," Murray said as he went into the kitchen to put on a pot of coffee. He and Dale had slipped on shorts but insisted Billy remain naked, a state of dress he loved.

"You really up for this?" Murray asked.

"You don't have to keep asking," Billy said, slightly annoyed. "If I wasn't, I wouldn't be here."

"I gotta say, Billy, that ass of yours is the best I've ever had. You're sitting on a fortune," Dale said,

Billy smirked. "Yeah, a lot of guys have told me that."

"You ever think of leaving Steve?" Dale asked.

"Why? You offering?"

Dale looked to Murray who nodded his head almost imperceptibly. "Maybe."

"You think you got what it takes to look after me? Satisfy my asshole?"

"Didn't you say we were the best?" Murray asked.

"Yeah, I did, didn't I?"

"Well?" Dale demanded.

"You'd let me fuck other guys? Fuck your friends?"

"Fuck, no!" Dale was adamant.

Billy shrugged that the conversation was over.

"Steve doesn't let you fuck his friends either," Murray pointed out.

Billy smiled. "But I do anyway."

Dale was so confident in his ability to satisfy Billy. "We'd keep you too busy. You wouldn't have the time."

"If you say so." Billy sounded bored. "You gonna invite Steve to the party?"

I held my breath. I didn't want my hiding place revealed because Billy would still think I was checking up on him and I wanted to see how true my closest friends were or whether they were turncoats like Dale and Murray.

Murray and Dale exchanged looks.

"I rang," Murray said. "No answer. I left a voicemail message. But I'll try him again once everyone arrives."

"You really want him to witness you being a fuck slut for all his closest friends?" Dale was trying to get his head around the idea. "You must really hate him."

"Nah, you don't understand."

Murray was curious. "What do you think he'll do if he catches you?"

"He could throw me out in the street." Billy seemed awfully calm about the prospect. "Or he can accept it, no questions asked."

"What, public humiliation? In front of his best friends? All fucking his lover?" Murray was incredulous at the prospect.

I began to think they'd forgotten I was in the closet listening to every word until there was a knock at the door and on his way to answer it, Dale distracted Billy's attention and Murray slipped me a cup of coffee. There's a lot to be said for civilized gay male behavior. They might have been cuckolding me by buggering my boyfriend in front of me but they remembered the social niceties. That goes a long way in my book. But not nearly far enough to make up for what they were doing. I didn't know whether they thought my non-intervention was passive acquiescence in their activity or whether I was just some poor cuckold who would tolerate his boyfriend's flagrant infidelity in a desperate attempt to keep him. They would be wrong on both counts.

The first to arrive was Kyle, who'd stopped off to pick up Jason, both guys who I went bar hopping with in my bachelor days. They heartily approved of Billy and had given no indication of having designs on his body. Kyle barged into the living room. "Lead me to him. I've heard so much about this pizza delivery guy I have to see him with my own eyes before I'll believe it."

"Hi Murray, Hi Billy," he called while he looked around. "Where is he? Don't tell me you've got him in the bedroom already? You cunning deviants!"

Dale smirked. "No, he's here in the room with us."

Jason looked about confused.

Billy drew his legs up on the lounge and parted them. A sly grin crept across Kyle's face. "Oh sweet Jesus. Tell me you're fuckin' serious, dude. Tell me I'm not dreaming."

Dale was as proud as if he was a new father. "You're not dreaming."

Kylie laughed. "Billy's the fuckin' pizza delivery boy? Man, this is so cool. Does Steve know?"

"Totally oblivious," Murray lied.

Jason needed reassurance. "He's gonna take us all on and you think Steve won't find out?"

Billy spoke for the first time since they arrived. "You care if he does?"

Kyle was adamant. "Fuck, no. I was only his friend so I could get my cock into you. I'm pretty bored because he won't let me near you."

"What about you, Jason?"

"I'm up for it. I've had sleepless nights dreaming about your butthole."

Billy seemed delighted. "Now I'm all yours. And yours."

He shifted so that his ass was easily accessible and Kyle didn't hesitate to shuck his clothes and had his cock aimed at Billy's pink ass chute before a slightly nervous Jason had even removed his shoes. I had to admire Kyle's body. He was buff. More buff than me and his cock was just the right length and thickness that Billy enjoyed. I saw him smile as Kyle slid in painlessly. They leaned in to kiss and Kyle was in no hurry to dump a load. Not now that he'd finally managed to nail the ass he'd obviously coveted for years.

While Jason moved closer so Billy could play with his cock, there was another knock at the door and Marty strode in. Marty was a prick. I worked with him. He was straight but I knew he'd always wanted to get into Billy. He tried it whenever my back was turned. He was certainly not on my friends list. Billy must have wanted him here for a reason. Surely not because he wanted his dick up his ass.

"Is that who I think it is?" Marty crowed as Dale handed him a drink. He looked skyward and whispered, "Thank you," before turning to the room and saying, "Now I know there really is a god."

He stripped down to his briefs, his middle-aged body hairy and out of shape. I saw Dale wrinkle his nose in distaste. He sat and watched while Kyle took his time fucking Billy smoothly and deeply. Jason straddled his face and sank his cock between Billy's lips.

Marty absent-mindedly played with his cock through his briefs. "Does Steve know about this little free-fuck-all?"

"It seems not," Kyle called over his shoulder. "Oh, Jesus, this ass is as good as they say. Fuckin' sweet. I could drill him all night."

"Yeah, well, you better hurry up because I want to pop my nuts real bad."

As if on cue, a few minutes later Kyle pushed hard against Billy and screwed up his face. "Ugh. Fuck. Shit. Fuck." It took him a few moments to get his breath back before he pulled out and Billy's fuckhole squelched. Jason had dismounted his face but Marty simply elbowed his way in and had his cock in Billy before Jason even had a chance.

"Hey, Marty, how would you like to fuck me in front of Steve?"

"Any time. I loathe everything that yuppie cunt stands for and would love to take him down. Thinks he's so fuckin' wonderful because he outsells the rest of us two to one."

"You'll tell all his co-workers you fucked me senseless?" Billy asked.

What Marty lacked in finesse he made up for in dogged determination.

"You bet I will. They'll fuckin' laugh at him every time he walks on the floor."

"Make sure you do," Billy said.

"Don't tell me what to do, cunt." Marty spat in Billy's face. It drooled down his cheek to his mouth. Billy poked at it with his tongue, licked it up, and then swallowed it.

"Nasty." Marty gobbed more spit directly into Billy's mouth. "Why don't I take you in the car yard, get everyone to line up and fuck your pretty little ass while Steve watches. Think he'd like that, Billy?"

"Who cares if he likes it?" Billy said.

"Oh, I do, Billy. I care a lot. I'd use you like a lump of fuck meat, show Steve who's boss. Who has the best cock, Billy?"

Billy groaned and I knew he was getting turned on. "You, Marty, you."

"Fuckin' right. Don't you ever forget it!" Marty couldn't seem to fuck and speak at the same time so he clammed up to concentrate on getting his rocks off. He grunted and sweated like an animal and the perspiration dripped into Billy's eyes. Eventually, he muttered "If I'd known how hot your ass is, I woulda thrown you down and fucked you in the street. Now I'm screwing your slutty faithless fuck hole," before letting fly with a string of expletives that made even Dale blush.

As soon as he pulled out, Jason sank into the slimy hole. Three more arrived but Nathan took one look at what was going on and froze. "Does Steve know about this?" he asked. When he was told that I didn't, he turned to Billy and said, "Much as I'd love to fuck you, mate, Steve is my friend. If he'd given permission I'd be up you like a rat up a drainpipe. But," he turned to everyone in the room, "He won't hear it from me." He closed the door as he left. One up for friendship. Not so, Spike, a tattoo punk that I'd befriended when I helped him get finance for a cheap van for his band.

Jason didn't take long to shoot with a barely audible moan and a slight judder of his body. Spike pulled him off Billy and pushed his own prick straight inside.

"So Steve is outa the loop?" he asked as he slammed back and forth, pulling his cock out fully before battering at Billy's sphincter again. I knew from experience it was the most painful way to fuck someone. But Billy was putting up with it. He almost looked as if he was welcoming the pain. Spike was hammering him into the lounge. "You gonna invite Stevie boy over for sloppy sevenths?"

"Would you like that, Spike?" Billy asked.

"Make him watch me nailing you to the floor. Let him see how you should be treated. Let him watch a real cock slam your sexy little body. That turn you on, Billy?"

Billy groaned and Spiked offered him his tattooed bicep. "Like the ink, boy? Worship the ink."

Billy's tongue snaked out and ran over the smooth skin of Spike's arm, and then he buried his nose and mouth in Spike's armpit, sucking and licking noisily, just as the last of the party arrived. Nick and Bryce arrived together and took one look at the well-fucked Billy before they decided they wanted in and shucked their clothes to join the pile on the floor.

"So this is the famed pizza boy everyone is talking about?" Bryce asked.

There was a chorus of agreement.

"Is he as good as the rumors?" Nick queried.

"A million fuckin' times better," Marty said.

"Shit, you'll make me come," Bryce groaned.

"So you all want to fuck Billy in front of Steve?" Dale had Billy's mobile phone in his hand.

A few of them looked startled but there's safety in numbers and they all agreed.

"I phoned him at home earlier this evening but he wasn't there. Let me try him again," Dale had an evil smile on his face.

I realized what he was planning, but I grabbed for my mobile too late, its distinctive ring tone echoing from my hiding place to the astonishment of all but Dale and Murray. With smug superiority Dale flung open the closet door to reveal me holding a cup of coffee in one hand and my hard cock in the other.

After a stunned silence, the laughter began. My humiliation was complete. Dale led me by the cock over to where Spike was still rough fucking Billy.

"Aren't you going to say hello to your boyfriend?" Dale asked.

"Hi, Billy," I muttered.

"Hi, Steve." Billy smiled. "Like what you see?"

Dale squeezed. "If his cock is anything to go by, I think Steve here likes to watch his boyfriend copping it good and hard. Why don't you just settle back and watch the fun, Steve? Who knows, maybe Billy will even let you join in. Or clean out his ass when we've finished."

"Gross," Marty called.

Dale turned to him. "What? You don't like the idea of your slimy cum that's fermenting in Bill's sloppy ass mixing with all ours then finally flushing down Steve's unwilling throat?"

Marty's eyes grew wide. "Now that you put it that way..."

There was no hiding my excitement while I sat and watched Billy fucked by each and every one of them, all declaring they'd never had an ass like it and, naturally enough, wanting seconds.

Billy drew the line at that. "Nah, guys. You got a preview tonight. And I was glad to give it to you. I love you guys fucking me and I can hardly wait to do it again." He went to his vest and took a handful of business cards from the pocket and handed them out. "You want another go then ring the number on the card. The code for what you want is printed on the back. I'll be glad to do anything you want. Anything at all."

The guys started to dress reluctantly.

"You gonna let Steve fuck you?" Marty asked.

"Hell, no. Not after I had the best fucks ever tonight from you guys. That would be an anti-climax. But can you get Steve to help clean me up?"

I could see they would enjoy this. They manhandled me to the floor and lay me down so Billy could squat over my face. Billy pushed his greasy ass cheeks down on to my face and rubbed the slime all over my nose, my forehead and my cheeks. I saw his sphincter strain and a small dribble of cum oozed down over the underside of his balls. Dale held on to my nose so I had to open my mouth. Billy strained again and a large chunk of cum shot out and onto my face. Dale rubbed it in and spooned it into my mouth. The dribble had become a cascade and cum oozed non-stop until I could scarcely keep it all in my mouth.

"Don't you dare swallow it," Billy commanded. "I want to see your best friends' cum all over your tongue. Swirl it around, Steve."

I did as I was told, the slime oozing down the back of my throat. I opened my mouth wide, poking out my tongue. He swapped positions, plugging my mouth with his own, suctioning up all the spooge. While looking down at me, he dribbled the snowball back again, spitting the remnant before he told me to swallow. My stomach heaved as the slime ran down into my gullet, but I kept it down.

I sat in a corner until the visitors left reluctantly and somewhat embarrassed, not knowing how to react to me now that they'd made their intentions clear about Billy. It probably hadn't sunk in as yet that I'd heard everything they'd said. I was sure guilt would set in before lunch tomorrow.

I got dressed quickly. "You want a lift, Billy?"

"Oh, yeah. Just sit in a corner until I finish with these two."

Murray was surprised. "You want more?"

"Sure, didn't I promise you two a turn off the clock?"

Murray stuttered. "Yeah, but I thought—"

"Well, don't," Billy said sharply. "When I say something I mean it. Steve can sit and watch while you two do me again. Maybe he can tell me what a slut I am and how you can fuck my ass until I can't stand up."

As it worked out, that's exactly what happened. I watched my two best friends work Billy over and got to verbally abuse my boyfriend while he cuckolded me, blowing a load in my trousers without even touching myself.

About half an hour later, I followed Billy in the van back to the depot, then he jumped in our car for the drive home. Neither of us spoke about what had just happened and when we got back to the apartment Billy said "Night," and went into his room closing the door.

I spent a very restless night, jerking off to the memory of all I'd seen.

Billy obviously intended keeping his pizza delivery job because he went out each evening and came back in the early hours of the morning reeking of cum and piss. I tried to speak to him about his behavior but he wouldn't countenance it. I was prepared to allow him certain leeway but fucking the men I considered my friends was beyond acceptable bounds even in my lapse moral code.

I got caught up in the cycle of overtime and mortgage repayments, utility bills and supermarket shopping and my resolve waivered. Billy realized we had to speak some time, and Sunday afternoons, before he headed out to work, became the time that he handed over his wages as I attempted to balance the books. I never queried the small amounts he gave me. He was either on a lousy hourly rate and the tips were not as abundant as he'd expected, men taking advantage of his good nature, or he was salting the money away, perhaps toward a nest egg to leave me and branch out on his own.

On one such Sunday in late November, Billy startled me with a request. "Next Sunday, can you to drive me to Uncle Ram's? It's the company Christmas party. He likes us all to be there."

"What time?"

"Leave mid-morning. To arrive in time for lunch."

Billy had never been close to this side of his family and we had never been invited to share Christmas or any other holiday with them before. Ram owned a house on the south coast at Coalcliff, about ninety minutes from the city, perched on top of a small bluff with its own private beach and a series of rock ledges from which the fishing was plentiful.

"Is the invitation for one or for two?"

"I didn't think you'd be interested," Billy replied. "It will be all my work colleagues. Mainly girls, and a few suppliers. It'll be a bit boring."

"Why are you going then?"

"It's...um...like mandatory. Uncle Ram gives out Christmas bonuses and unless you've got a very good reason for not attending, like death, you don't get it. Plus there are prizes for best delivery girl, best feedback from customers, and all the usual sort of shit."

"The prize being a voucher for one of his own pizzas no doubt." I was thinking of how stingy Billy's wages had been and I couldn't see the bonus or the prizes adding up to much.

Billy shrugged his indifference. "Can you do it? Otherwise I'll have to hire a car to get there."

"What about one of your customers? Dale or Murray could drive you." I regretted saying it the moment the words left my mouth.

Billy sighed. "Uncle Ram doesn't allow fraternization between customers and staff."

"At the Christmas party at any rate," I added.

"Look, forget it. It's no big deal. I'll see if anyone can give me a lift. I only thought it might be a nice change for you. When you're not at work, which seems to be all the time, you're cooped up inside the apartment trying to balance the books..."

I bit my tongue. No use in starting an argument.

"You can go swimming, do a bit of rock fishing, or just relax for the afternoon," Billy continued. "We can drive back when you've had enough. It will do you good."

"You want me to come then?"

"I was afraid you might be bored. If you don't want to, that's your choice, I'll stay overnight, there's no work that night, all the franchises are closed for the party, and hitch a ride back with someone in the morning."

It did sound inviting. I'd been on my guard only because I thought it may have been yet another opportunity for Billy to get himself into situations that would lead to my ultimate humiliation. I didn't think my blood pressure could stand it. The way our relationship was headed, this would be our last Christmas together – if it lasted until then – and I thought we might as well make the most of it. I might even be able to get him drunk and take advantage of him myself. My balls were turning blue from lack of sex. All my overtures to Billy had been rebuffed since he'd begun work at Pizza with Everything.

I couldn't help one last snipe. "Okay, I'll drive you up and drive you back, as long as you don't think I'll cramp your style."

Billy shook his head at my clumsy put down and went to his room, closing the door, emerging only a few hours later to head off to work without even saying goodbye. A few more weeks of this cold shoulder and they'd be locking me up.

The rest of the week passed in much the same way, Billy avoiding me, which wasn't all that difficult given our overlapping work schedules, and me tucking him in and kissing him secretly each morning before heading out, smelling other men's sex on his face and body.

Billy thawed a little by the following weekend, so the scheduled party run was going ahead. Ram was supplying all the food, free beer and soft drinks, plus a fruit punch, and a little home-made grappa which I'd heard was lethal. I packed a half dozen bottles of quality wine to help out, grateful that all gifts, except alcohol, were strictly verboten. Ram would play Santa Claus and distribute small gifts to the children of his employees and the few relatives who still acknowledged his branch of the family tree.

I drove the car out of the underground parking bay and waited for Billy in the street. Okay, we've been together almost six years now, but even I had to whistle when he appeared and hopped into the passenger's seat. He looked gorgeous. He'd obviously spent a little of his wages on new casual clothes and he certainly knew how to pick garments that brought out his coloring and the beauty of his muscular body and his handsome face. I fell in love with him all over again. He seemed pleased at my reaction and the smile stayed on his face for the next twenty minutes.

I swore to myself I would do and say nothing to spoil the day, no matter the provocation, although I was not expecting much from this family-oriented event. The ninety-minute trip was pleasant, I enjoy driving, although the conversation was sparse. The radio proved a source of irritation and our small talk, we avoided the personal, dried up very quickly, so that for most of the journey Billy listened to his iPod via his ear pieces and gazed silently out the window at the passing scenery.

As the highway wound down the coast we came across spectacular views of the Pacific and the vast expanse of blue ocean lifted my spirits, dulled somewhat by Billy's uncommunicative behavior. When we finally arrived and turned into the driveway of Ram's house, we both were shocked by the opulence. The gravel driveway led up to a two-story white mansion with marble columns pretentiously framing the magnificent carved oak front door. The residence glistened in the hot and humid midday sun, vehicles already clogging the parking spots although I managed to squeeze the car into one of the few remaining spaces. Carrying the box of wine we headed to the door which opened just before we had a chance to ring.

"Billy, glad you could make it. We were just about to send out a search party. How's my favorite nephew?" Ram was a big bear of a man in his late forties, who'd obviously eaten a little too readily of his own product. He was a good 280lbs and stood 6'2". Billy disappeared into his hug. I thought the big man would suffocate him.

He turned his attention to me and almost crushed the bones in my hand he shook it so vehemently. "You must be Steve, we've heard so much about you. Glad to finally meet you. Billy never stops praising your finer points."

I knew he was just being polite but I was surprised to see that Billy had a smut of red in his cheeks.

"Hello, I'm Ruby. Welcome to our family. Glad you could make our little party."

Billy leaned in and kissed her on the cheek. "Hello, Auntie Ruby." She, too, enveloped him in her arms and pressed him to her very large artificially enhanced breasts. Ruby, alias porn royalty Clitty Glitter, whom I had seen gang banged and double penetrated by twelve men in *Orgy on the Orient Express*, was a stunning woman. She still managed the occasional non-sexual guest appearance in hetero porn although it was rumored she was the body double on a number of recent best sellers when the lead actress was unable to accommodate men of, shall we say, extra-large proportions. She also guested as harridan mums and girlfriends in gay porn where she had attracted a cult following.

Her long red hair, her crowning glory and, along with triple penetration, her trademark, was truly spectacular. More impressive yet was the adoring way in which she looked at her husband. This truly was a love match. She hugged me as tightly as she did Billy. She smelled of apricots and popcorn. I liked her immediately and felt right at home.

The wine was taken from me and Ruby walked us out amongst the guests who were already swimming in the pool or else sitting about in groups chatting on the mansion's expansive ground-level entertaining area. A number of young women screamed when they saw Billy, rushing over to claim him, stripping him to his Speedos before dragging him to the pool where they carried on like a bunch of kids.

Ruby took my arm, introducing me to the men, most of whom were the boyfriends of the female pizza delivery crew. I wondered how they coped with their girlfriends' infidelity. The remainder of the guests were cooks and general hands at the pizza franchises, plus a smattering of suppliers. "Billy really is a remarkable young man," Ruby said.

"Yes," I replied non-committally.

She stopped to look at me. "You must be something special the way he talks about you."

"I didn't know he'd been here before," I said.

"Oh, no, he hasn't. I help out in the shop. Sometimes I do the deliveries for old times' sake, when Ram is in one of his shitty moods."

My face must have given me away. "Now, I've shocked you." She laughed and led me along to meet another group of guests.

She left me while she went in to help prepare lunch. I had to admit it was fun standing chatting amiably with a group of strangers not having to worry about Billy. Children raced around screaming, getting tangled amongst the adults, while the beer and wine flowed, as did the bonhomie. I wandered away to look at the superb garden of native plants that had a precarious existence here on the cliff top, buffeted by easterlies that swept in off the salty sea.

I found a sun lounge and sat to watch Billy frolicking in the pool. He waved happily and I saluted him with my drink in acknowledgement. He was the center of attention among the young women, some of whom surreptitiously groped his ass while a few squeezed his cock. He batted them away good naturedly; otherwise I would have suspected he had bisexual tendencies.

Life was good today. I dreaded to think of our return to the city where Billy would once again take refuge in the spare room. If only he would tell me what the problem was, I was sure we could overcome it.

A shadow obstructed the sun. "You must be Billy's boyfriend."

Shading my eyes I looked up. He was very cute. Mediterranean. Greek, Italian, perhaps Lebanese. He was clothed only in Speedos which did little to disguise the size of his cock.

"Steve." I held out my hand as he sat in the lounge chair beside me.

"Mario. This your first time?"

"Uh huh."

"Your Billy is very popular. And not just here. Natasha...that's her in the red," he said pointing to a stunning blonde who was all over Billy. "She fancies him something fearful. She's tried but she got nowhere."

I smiled. "I think she'll find she lacks the equipment that Billy needs."

"She even offered to wear a strap-on."

I laughed. "That is keen." I looked over at him. "You don't mind?"

He looked serious. "Sometimes. What about you?"

"I was never given a choice."

"Ouch."

We sat and watched the pool. Shortly Ram came out and spoke to Natasha. She got out and dried herself, shaking her wet hair, and waved to Mario before disappearing inside the house.

"What was that all about?" I enquired.

"She was chosen."

"Chosen?"

"Yeah. It's no big deal. The cops turn up throughout the day for their annual pay off. As a special Christmas bonus, Ram lets them choose one of the girls, only the delivery chicks not the wives or anything, for a special in one of the bedrooms. Sometimes they even choose Ruby. It's all very democratic. You can only get chosen once."

He seemed very casual about the process.

"Well, I suppose Billy doesn't have much chance."

"Don't you believe it. Tash tells me he's one of the most popular delivery staff they've ever had. Some of the girls are losing customers to him. Straight guys who want to try it out."

"Like you?"

He chuckled. "How did you know?"

"Easy. That rather lethal looking weapon you've got barely hidden in your Speedos twitches every time you mention his name."

"Why, Steve, are you staring at my cock?"

"If you don't want people to stare at it you shouldn't be wearing those trunks."

"You don't mind, do you?"

"Wouldn't matter if I did. Billy is his own man. But, no, I don't mind. Doesn't mean I wouldn't be as envious as hell. You're a hot fucker."

"You think he'd be interested?"

"With that tantalizing bulge you've got, I think Billy would be bending over in a matter of seconds. I'm surprised you haven't porked him already."

"I never saw him before today. He certainly lives up to all the hype."

"Don't I know it."

"If I get a chance at his ass, Tash wants to watch."

I didn't like her chances.

The lunch went off without a hitch and Billy stayed glued to my side, giving the appearance that we were the happiest couple alive. He was almost like his old self, discussing fantasy partnering, picking out men at the party he'd like to fuck 'if he were single.' I wasn't sure if that qualification about bachelorhood was a threat about the parlous state of our relationship or a confirmation that we were still in one. I didn't dare ask because that was territory he didn't wish to explore at the moment.

He picked out a handful of men who had taken his fantasy, all straight, or so he maintained.

"What about Mario? He's very attractive and seems to have quite a handful down his Speedos."

"I've sort of put him out of my mind because he's Tash's boyfriend," Billy said.

"Hmmm, that never stopped you from fucking my best friends," I pointed out. I knew I shouldn't have said it, but I was still bitter. To cover my faux pas I added quickly, "Besides, it's not like she's exactly faithful. Isn't she fucking for tips when she delivers pizza?"

Billy paused to consider what I'd said. "You think he'd be interested?"

"Definitely. But only if Tash can watch."

Billy grimaced. "Not sure I'm up for that. Particularly as I think she'd probably try to join in at some stage."

Because it was so hot and humid in the garden, most of the guests remained in their swimming costumes, including Billy who was getting more than his share of admiring glances, from men as well as women.

"What's the schedule for this afternoon?" I asked.

"Ram will come out dressed as Santa Claus shortly. He'll give gifts to all the kids who are here then we go through that rigmarole I told you about earlier. He gets the delivery girls to sit on his knee. He gives the prettiest girls a quick feel, nothing too blatant otherwise Ruby would have his balls, he gives them their bonus and they give him a sloppy kiss and then the next one takes a turn. Before that there's a short ceremony where he hands out prizes for best pizza cook, best pizza delivery, that sort of shit."

"Are you in the running?"

"We all are. It's democratic. Nobody votes or anything. It goes by sales, or workload or the public writing in, that sort of thing. As for me, I don't stand a snowball's. I've only worked there three months. The job is over on Christmas Eve."

"You're giving it away? I thought you liked it?"

"Whatever gave you that idea?" Billy asked.

"I just thought—"

I was saved further embarrassment when Christmas carols blared out over the sound system set up in the barbecue area, and Ram made his appearance dressed in a heat-stroke inducing Santa outfit. Pandemonium broke out as kids squealed and ran to him and his big sack of goodies. Each gift had been especially hand-picked to the taste of the recipient. I was amazed at the trouble to which he'd gone to get things right. Perhaps I had misjudged him.

With the kids safely out of the way and moved to a special part of the garden, under the care of a nanny specifically hired for the occasion to give the parents a respite, Ram got down to the real business of the day. He called for quiet and his workers gathered around him in expectation of cash and the chance at a prize. There was a scattering of applause as names totally unfamiliar to me were called out and prizes awarded.

I had to admit Ram was a more generous employer than I had anticipated. Cash prizes were substantial without being ridiculous, but as Billy was eligible in only one category, pizza delivery, and unlikely to win I didn't pay much attention.

Bored guests with no financial or emotional interest in the proceedings drifted off for the afternoon's activities. The men for a booze-up on the beach, the women for a natter and their own space around the pool. There were no hard and fast rules and the sexes could mix if they wished but Ruby told me they kept pretty much to their own domains, until late afternoon when they came together for their farewells.

I joined her in the kitchen to help with the tidy up after the meals. The sound of people slamming their hands down on the wooden furniture and whoops of delight and shrill whistles signaled the event was over. I changed into my swimming togs and headed outside with my beach towel fully intending to take advantage of the sun. I found Billy and he suggested I join the exodus but that he would have to stay until he received his bonus. He looked terribly disappointed so I knew he must have expected to take out one of the prizes. I doubted they had one for the biggest slut or the delivery boy most likely to humiliate his boyfriend.

There was something in the way he suggested I leave, as well as that tell-tale look of guilt when he suggested I would be bored that held me there. I had walked away as if taking Billy's advice but lingered at the back of the crowd out of his view.

The dispensing of Ram's largesse was a tedious and lengthy business. He took pride of place at a large table which had an assortment of envelopes on it. Now that the kids had been shepherded out of sight, he'd removed his Santa outfit except for the boots, his Santa cap and a pair of red shorts. He was a striking looking man, not exactly fat but not exactly buff either. The cooks and general hands were disposed of quickly. A kind word of thanks and encouragement, a quick handshake and an envelope of cash was all it took. It was only when he got to the pizza delivery girls that things got rowdy, and other women made a hasty exit.

The atmosphere got decidedly bawdy, male guests whooping and hollering drunkenly as the girls sat on Ram's knee while he pretended to finger them then sniff and lick his hand, while he made sexist comments about their figures and their loose morals. He was very specific about their expertise in certain sexual proclivities and guests would slap the girl's boyfriend on the back to show their appreciation of her skills. A few of the girls giggled when it was their turn, one shrieked in surprise, and one or two had glazed eyes by the time they got off his lap.

I thought Billy would get a quick hand shake and we'd be on our way. But no, Billy sat on Ram's knee, placing his arms around his uncle's neck to whisper in his ear. There were catcalls and cheers until Ram raised his hands for quiet.

"Billy here, has surprised us all with the amount of business he has generated for the company. Plus the unlimited goodwill. Let's not forget it's his unrelenting hard work that has, in part, been responsible for the larger than usual Christmas bonus you've received this year."

A few of the girls called out their support for Billy, while their boyfriends grumbled.

"So what is it about Billy? Well, we polled our clients, and they tell us it's this." Ram patted Billy's butt cheeks, leaving his big meaty hand there. "So, I thought I'd better inspect the goods myself to see what's so special about it."

A few of the guests squirmed and moved off.

"There's your bonus on the table, Billy. Lean over and get it."

Billy did as he was told and assumed the position. He was bent forward reaching for the envelope when Ram pulled down his Speedos and quickly simulated shoving his fingers into Billy's delectable rear. No wonder he'd wanted me to be absent from this display. I was probably the only person to see the look cloud Billy's face. This was no simulation, this was real. Ram had his fingers embedded in his nephew's ass. He pulled them free and pushed them into Billy's mouth.

"Hmm," he purred. "Feels so good."

"Why don't you fuck him?" someone yelled from the crowd.

Ram smiled, and it was not a pretty sight. "You think I should."

The chant went up. "Fuck him! Fuck him! Fuck him!"

Ram rubbed his body against Billy's ass and a roar went up. They didn't want reality, they just wanted ritual humiliation.

"Feels so good," Ram said.

"Harder, make him squeal," someone else shouted.

Someone disagreed. "That's sick, man."

In the seconds that people's attention was turned to the naysayer, I saw Ram pull out his cock. Billy's cry of surprise and pain, and the startled look in his eyes, was a dead giveaway, at least to me, that Ram had his cock in Billy's hole. He pretended like he was riding Billy but he was, in reality, up to his balls in his nephew's butt. Gross! Billy really had hit the gutter with an act like this.

As a few of the guests realized this was a real butt fucking, they turned to see if I was in the audience. Billy saw me watching him from the back of the crowd and attempted to push Ram off, but his uncle held him firmly around the waist until he closed his eyes and leaned his head back, his mouth opening, and he shuddered briefly. A few moments later Billy adjusted his swimming costume and headed over to me, leaving his envelope with his uncle for safekeeping.

I made no mention of what I had just seen, and Billy behaved as if nothing untoward had happened, ignoring the fact he had just added illegal activity to immoral behavior.

On the beach proper, a thin strip of sand the size of a pocket handkerchief, the men were playing cricket, so we joined Mario sun bathing on the rock shelf that jutted out into the ocean. We'd seen him from the cliff top, lying in his knee-length black shorts soaking up rays. He was glad of the company and, I suspect, the opportunity to put the moves on Billy.

The two of them kept the conversation going, mainly about comic incidences within the pizza company, something that bored me so I fell asleep. That would also give Mario the opportunity to try his darnedest to win over my boyfriend. It was someone calling Billy's name that woke me from my slumber. Ram's right-hand man had turned up. "Billy, I hate to do it so late in the day, but you've been, um..." he looked at me before going on. "You've been chosen."

"Aw, shit. I'm enjoying myself here. Can't you tell them I've gone home or something?" he pleaded.

"Nah, special request."

"Okay, I'll be right up."

Billy turned to me and, not realizing I knew what being one of the chosen meant, and made his excuses. "Something I've gotta do for Ram. Sorry. But it should only take half an hour or so. I'll be back before you know it."

"That's okay, I'll still be here." I lay back down on my towel.

After Billy had gone, Mario turned to me, "At least he didn't lie."

"He didn't quite tell the truth either," I said. "If you hadn't told me what it meant, I could have spent the afternoon blissfully unaware. As it is now, I have a knot in my stomach."

The party just became a little less relaxing and a great deal more tense.

Mario looked at me. "Sorry. I shouldn't have told you."

"I would have found out."

"I've got an idea," Mario said. "Why don't we go peek at what's happening? If I can't get Billy's ass for real why not watch it in action, second-best thing."

The idea certainly had merit. I wouldn't be exposed as a voyeur, and he wouldn't be fucking with anyone I knew, especially friends of mine, and I do like watching Billy in action. I guess it's a win/win situation. Besides, my cock was hard as the gravel in the mansion driveway.

Leaving our towels where they were we raced for the stairs. Billy had already disappeared so he would not notice us shadowing him.

"They set a couple of the spare bedrooms aside for these little Christmas bonus bribes and they all have glass doors that open on to a private central courtyard. I know a secret way in. There's plenty of bush and scrub to hide behind so we can watch."

The more I thought about it the more excited I became. No one took any notice of us as we passed the swimming pool going toward the house and we managed to detour down the side passageway without being seen. A high brick wall fenced off the fourth side of the courtyard. I didn't know how we were going to get inside, it was certainly too difficult to scale. The wooden door to the garden was locked and bolted. Checking to see if anyone was watching, Mario carefully manhandled one of the blocks of sandstone that held the door lock in place. It lifted out and the door swung open.

"You sly bastard," I whispered. "You've done this before."

We could hear voices so we propped the door closed before crawling our way across the yard for a better view into the bedroom. The glass doors were open for ventilation in the humid weather, the curtains drawn back to allow what little breeze there was off the sea to infiltrate the room to cool it down. The occupants had no reason to believe they had anything but absolute privacy. The doors to the other rooms were closed and, I assumed, locked. The courtyard was private and there were no upstairs windows on this side of the house. It had been created for secrets.

We found a position where we could sit on the paving stones and look directly into the bedroom.

"Okay, where's the guy I'm supposed to entertain? I want to get this over with and go back to Steve," I heard Billy say. He was seated on the edge of the double bed still in his swimming costume. Ram was pacing.

"Your boyfriend doesn't have a fuckin' clue, does he?" Ram chuckled.

"He's not stupid. He'll catch on quick enough."

"You know you're the most successful pizza delivery...um...person we've ever had. If we could clone you we'd retire millionaires. We have people ringing up begging us to send you over, to be added to the waiting list in case of cancellation. Why would you want to give that up?"

"You wouldn't understand."

"Try me."

"We've had this conversation. I'm not going to change my mind."

"We'll see."

"Okay, if that's what you want to believe." Billy sounded tired. "So where is he?"

"Right here."

"You?"

"Think of it as research. I gotta find out what your secret is so I can repeat it with other guys when you retire."

"Jesus Christ, Ram, you're my uncle. Isn't that illegal?"

"You owe me this much."

"I don't owe you anything. You already fucked me in public. In front of Steve. Okay, so everyone else thought you were kidding around but you and I know the truth." Billy started for the door but Ram grabbed him by the arm and threw him down.

"Holy fuckin' shit," Mario whispered. "What are we going to do?"

"Nothing at all, unless it gets violent," I replied. "Billy can look after himself."

There was no way, even with his muscle development that Billy could overcome Ram's pure brute strength.

"That little quickie outside was just a taste, an entrée. I want the full menu."

"What's to stop me screaming for help?"

"No one will hear you. These rooms are soundproofed."

"What if I accuse you of rape?"

"By the time I've finished with you, you'll be begging for more. No one will believe a slut. Your reputation precedes you."

Ram grabbed Billy by the hair and dragged him to edge of the bed then shucked off his shorts, kicking them aside, his hard cock close to Billy's face.

"What's the big deal, Billy? You've sucked nastier cocks than mine."

"I wasn't related to them."

"I thought that would be an extra bonus, Billy. You take after my side of the family. Look at my cock, boy. Like it?"

Ram was a pretty impressive sight for his age. Naked he was the sort of man Billy loved to dominate him. Big, solid body with a smattering of hair on his chest and stomach and a little on his shoulders, his cock was a long, thick uncircumcised barge pole. The length would not trouble Billy, but the circumference would test both his holes capacity to expand.

"Shit, I think he's going to do it," Mario whispered.

"Of course he's going to do it," I whispered back. "Billy can't resist a cock like that."

Billy looked conflicted. "If only you weren't my uncle."

Ram lifted his nephew's chin up so that they looked each other in the eye. "You can pretend I'm someone else if you want to but it would be a shame to deny yourself the exquisite torture. Don't you feel that sick sensation of excitement in your stomach?"

"I get that whenever I know I'm doing something bad. Or something that will totally humiliate Steve. Like fucking with his best friends."

"It's a powerful aphrodisiac. Embrace it, Billy."

Ram was slowly milking his cock, peeling the foreskin back, rubbing his thumb around the piss slit. Billy was mesmerized.

"It's so nasty. So forbidden. That's why you want to do it. Reach out and touch your uncle's cock, Billy."

Billy wrapped his hand around the hard prick but withdrew it like he'd touched burning coals.

"Take your Speedos off, Billy. Get down on your knees and smell my cock and balls."

Billy did as he was told, sinking naked to his knees to sniff Ram's balls.

"What would Steve want you to do if he was here watching this right now?"

Billy looked up at the mountain of a man towering over him. "He'd want me to worship your cock, Uncle Ram."

Ram reached under the pillow on the bed, retrieving a bottle of poppers hidden there. He uncapped it and took two long snorts before holding it out for Billy to sniff.

"Here, Billy, though I don't think you need it." Billy sniffed like he was vacuuming courage out of the bottle.

Ram capped it and put it on the bedside table within easy reach. It was only a matter of moments before the drug kicked in.

"Come on, nephew, lick under the foreskin. Lick your uncle's hard cock, lick it, that's right, slowly boy, want to make this last. Watching your mouth slide along my shaft...your aunt can suck like a Hoover but she can't give blow jobs for shit, porn star or no porn star. Not like your mouth, Billy."

Billy came up for air. "But she's one of the most famous in the business."

Ram ran his hands through Billy's blond locks. "On screen, Billy, she's a whore; at home, she can be a bit of a puritan. You getting off on this, aren't you, Billy?"

"Fuck, yeah, uncle Ram. I've always wanted to suck your cock, feel it fill my mouth since you used to come over to my dad's place. I used to watch you when you showered. I wanted to go down on my knees and blow you until you dumped in my sweet throat."

"Pity we left it so long then, nephew."

Ram picked up the bottle, handing it to Billy who snorted six times before relinquishing it to Ram who followed suit.

"Open wide, Billy, this will tickle your tonsils."

Ram grabbed the back of his head and began to push his thick cock into Billy's gob. His lips stretched to take it, his eyes watered, he gagged. Ram pulled back a little before pushing it farther and farther toward Billy's throat. I could see Billy regulating his breathing to take it. The amyl had relaxed him and he seemed determined to take it all even if his jaw was dislocated in the process.

"Fuck, your mouth is so warm, nephew. Just a little bit more. That's it, boy. Take it all. Think how proud Steve would be if he saw you swallow your uncle's big, fat prick right down to the root."

That did it! Billy made one last valiant attempt to house the monster. His face was full of cock, his lips straining to take it, his throat raw, his eyes ablaze, and his nose running with a little snot.

"Fuck, nephew, you did it! Not many have ever taken me down to the balls."

Billy had no intention of letting it rest there. He reached for the poppers; slowly taking his mouth off the shaft to rest his jaw, snorted, and then handed the phial to Ram. Once the fumes reached his brain, Billy slammed his mouth over the huge gleaming prick, tickling and squeezing Ram's balls as he pummeled his own face.

"Oh, shit, nephew. Shit. I've never had anyone fuck my cock with their mouth like you're doing." Ram stumbled, almost losing his footing under Billy's oral onslaught and the effects of the amyl. "Suck it, you dirty little cunt," Ram snarled. "Take your uncle's cock right down that slut throat. Want to drown in your uncle's spunk? I bet you do, Billy. Want me to shoot down your throat? All over your face? Leave my uncle spunk in your asshole?"

I eased my prick out of my swimming costume to give it a chance to breathe; it was so hot and hard. I milked it slowly as I watched my boyfriend's debasement at the hands of his uncle.

Billy gagged, spluttered, pulled off and gasped for air before ramming his face down on the slimy cock.

Ram held his head and began to take control, he had to be close. Suddenly, he gasped loudly, held Billy's face embedded fully on his prick, and screamed, "Holy fuckin' mother of god."

Billy's throat was bobbing as the sperm shot down into his gullet. He attempted to push Ram off but he was held tight in a headlock. I was afraid for a moment he would pass out but Ram finally released him and Billy sat back on the floor, his breath ragged, his chin a mixture of spunk and puke, his nose running and his eyes filled with the tears of near choking.

"Fuck, that was intense," he managed to gasp.

Ram flopped back on the bed. "Shit, no wonder you were so popular. And if your ass is as half as good as your mouth I'd be tempted to turn for you, Billy."

Compliments always worked. Billy smiled. "Not half as good, Uncle Ram. Twice as good. And I hope you're gonna find out for yourself shortly."

Ram lifted him on to the bed and flipped him on his belly so he could run his hands over Billy's sweet ass. He pressed his fingers at the puckered hole and then moved across the room to get lube from one of the drawers. He passed the bottle of poppers to Billy. "You may need this, unless you've taken a baseball bat up your ass before. I only got half inside earlier. I want my cock balls deep in you this time."

Billy arched his butt making it easier for Ram to pour lube down his crack and massage it into his receptive hole. Billy groaned his appreciation as Ram pushed two fingers inside. Any of his fingers was equal to an average size cock so Billy was being stretched.

"Open me up like this, Uncle Ram, and then flip me on my back. I want to watch your face as you hammer me."

"Good boy. You know, I could get to like this gay shit. Seems to me you're a lot less squeamish than the girls I got on the books. You're game for anything. Maybe I should organize a poker night with some of the boys for you. Without Steve, of course. Think he'd let you out for the night? Of course, you'd be the meat in the sandwich."

"I think Steve might let me, especially if we don't tell him you guys are gonna tag my ass."

Billy knew me too well.

"You opened up enough?"

"Hell, yeah," Billy said, pushing back on to the invading fingers.

"That is one superb ass," Mario said attempting to adjust his cock in his bathers.

Without so much as a 'by your leave', Ram lined up the head of his prodigious weapon against Billy's tiny hole and pushed.

"Holy fuck!" Billy cried. "I can feel every fuckin' inch of that monster."

"You'll get used to it, nephew."

And he did. After a few minutes of Ram plunging his prick in and out of his guts, Billy began to push back to take as much as he could.

"Looks as if you're ready for the hammering of your young life," Ram said, pulling out and flipping Billy over. He pushed Billy's legs up until his knees were against his shoulders. "Boy, you've got no idea how much I've been looking forward to this moment."

Billy raised the bottle to his nose and took a mammoth hit. He threw his head back as the rush hit him. "Fuck my tight little nephew boy cunt, Uncle Ram. Make me scream. Fuck me until I can't stand up."

The rhythm was slow and gentle at first but Billy must have been doing his trick with his ass muscles and Ram uttered little yelps each time he sank his shaft into Billy's chute. He picked up the pace. "You like a bit of uncle cock, Billy? Feels so good knowing you're the son of my cunt brother. Bet he'll shit himself when he hears I fucked his little boy up the ass. Screwed his brains out. Fucked him till he couldn't stand up."

There was something repulsive yet cock hardening watching this guy bend his own nephew over and slam into him. Mario must have thought so, too, as he released his own cock and sighed. "This is so fuckin' intense, man. So sick. So nasty. I gotta jerk off."

Much as I wanted to watch Billy being screwed into the bed, Mario's cock was too good to waste. I shifted my body closer and put my mouth over his drooling prick. He hadn't noticed and gasped when he felt my warm wet tongue. I thought for a moment he might push me away but he took his hand off his shaft and let me go to work while he watched the live action in the bedroom in front of us.

I got only the soundtrack now and it consisted of totally filthy talk with Billy and Ram daring each other in more and more perverse language, more and more depraved fantasies which I'm sure, given half a chance they both would have eagerly enacted. I was pleased to see that I featured heavily in most of them. And, not to be too modest about it, I would have gladly joined in. In fact, I was tempted to stand up and walk into the bedroom now, except for one tiny fact, well not-so-tiny really, Mario's cock.

"You cheap whore, you fuckin' piece of slut meat, feel my cock pounding your asshole, Billy?"

"I want to be your cock whore, Uncle Ram. Feel you bang my nephew cunt."

They were both so sex crazed at the moment I don't think they would have noticed if the world had come to an end.

There was silence except for the sound of two bodies slamming together. Mario groaned softly, "That is so fuckin' gross," and shot his load into my mouth.

I swallowed as quickly as I could and then sat up to see what had caused the outburst. Ram had leaned in to kiss Billy and uncle and nephew were in the throes of the most passionate lip lock I could imagine.

That was enough for Ram to lose it and I saw his body shudder as he shot his cum inside Billy's ass. When they finally separated I saw Billy had shot a load as well as it oozed down his stomach.

They both lay back on the bed exhausted. I thought they may have been embarrassed by what they had done but the first thing Ram said was, "You just gotta come to Christmas dinner here so I can fuck you again."

"I usually go to Steve's parents' place for Christmas but your invitation is much more inviting. Steve can drop me off on his way through."

"He won't mind?"

"Probably, but I want that monster up my butt again as soon as possible."

"Don't forget that poker night."

"That's if Steve lets me."

"Make sure he does. I want to see that look on your face again when I fuck your ass."

Mario and I sneaked back out of the courtyard as they dressed. We headed back to the beach and I gathered up our belongings, returning to the house as Billy emerged from the bedroom. He was happy to leave, he looked flushed and exhausted, and we made our farewells before heading to the car.

We fought all the way home about Billy not coming to my family's usual Christmas celebration and we both said things we later regretted. The chill in our relationship continued right through until Christmas day and, in fact, right up until I dropped him back at Ram's mansion. He didn't bother to say goodbye and I didn't bother giving him his Christmas present. I was so angry I could scarcely drive.

I was about fifty km up the highway when my mobile rang. I pulled over to the side of the road. I thought it was Billy ringing to apologize in which case I would back down as well and offer to come back a day early and pick him up. The caller ID showed that it wasn't.

"Hi, mum. Merry Christmas."

"Merry Christmas, son."

"What's up?" There was a long pause. "Has something happened?"

"No, no. Nothing like that."

"What is it then?"

"I don't quite know how to put this," mum said.

"Come on, spit it out, it can't be that bad."

"Of course not." I heard her take a deep breath. "You are coming alone, aren't you? That slutty boyfriend of yours is not with you, is he?"

I was shocked. "Pardon me?"

"That Billy character. You're not bringing him, are you?"

I could scarcely hold my temper. "No, I told you, he's gone to his uncle's place. I dropped him off about half an hour ago."

"Good. I thought he might change his mind. He was rather rude on the phone."

"Um, when did you speak to him on the phone?"

"Let me see, about two months back, I think it was."

"Who rang whom?"

"I rang him, of course."

"Why?"

"To tell him he was not welcome here."

"Why would you tell him that?"

"I don't want to hurt your feelings, dear. But the boy's a slut. He's proud of it. It's even tattooed on his body. But I don't have to tell you that."

"Apart from the fact the tattoo was forced on him, why didn't you speak to me about this?"

"I thought your silly flirtation with this person would be well and truly over by now. That you would discover for yourself what sort of a person he is and throw him out."

"Just exactly what sort of a person is he, mum?"

"He's a degenerate, Steven. Need you ask?"

"Yes, I need to ask. So you rang and told him he wasn't welcome. What did he say?"

"Not much. He seemed to accept it."

"Did he ask why?"

"He knows why."

"Did he attempt to defend himself?"

"How could he? He said he would abide by my wishes. And then said he would find an excuse to stay away at Christmas. He would not tell you about my phone call because it would upset you. Something about not wanting to make you choose between him and his family, whatever that meant."

"You don't know what that means?"

"Not a clue, dear."

"Precisely where did you get this idea that Billy is a, uh, degenerate."

"Steven, it's really not the time to be discussing this. We can talk further when you arrive."

"No, mum. Now."

"Your father will tell you all about it when you get here. It's quite sickening. It turned my stomach. And your brother, too. How could he be so brazen? They didn't say anything when you both visited to spare your feelings, son."

"So, Billy what? Propositioned dad and Eddie? Is that it?"

"He tried to touch them. Tried to have his way with Eddie in his gym in the basement. And with your father, of all people. Your father was so revolted he wanted to vomit. They don't want to be put in that situation ever again."

"And you believe them?

Of course she did. She had to. Or else acknowledge her marriage was a sham and her son a liar.

She was indignant. "Of course I believe them."

"Is that the same father and brother that came to the city a few months back with their sports team and invited Billy along as their team mascot?"

"They explained that. It was for your sake."

"Okay, I get the picture, mum."

"Good. It's very distasteful. I don't know how your judgment could have been so awry. Let's just forget it and have a happy Christmas dinner."

"Why did you feel you needed to ring me about this now, mum?"

"Your father and your brother didn't want the embarrassment if he turned up unexpectedly."

"I'll bet they didn't."

"It almost sounds like you're taking that man's side."

"You know something, mum. I am. You and dad and Eddie have yourselves a happy little family Christmas because I'm turning the car around and I'm going to spend the day with my family. With Billy. I don't blame you, mum. I'm sorry you got involved. But if I have to take sides, then I'm siding with Billy. Sorry I won't make it home this year. Maybe next. Bye, mum."

I heard her shout, "Steven!" just before I disconnected and switched the phone off. I turned the car around and headed back toward Ram's place. Either destination had been problematic but I knew in which direction my heart lie. I was tempted to speed but I could ill-afford double demerits if I was caught.

It was the longest forty minute drive of my life. Ruby answered the door. "You'll find him down on the rocks." As I raced for the cliff stairs she called, "You'll be staying for lunch?"

"If you'll have me," I called back, hoping she heard me. I could swear I heard her chuckle in response.

I descended to the beach in record time, dreading that I would fall and injure myself in my haste, but I didn't want to waste a second getting to the man I loved. As I trudged through the sand toward the rock ledge I saw him sitting staring out to sea. I crept up and had my arms around him before he was even aware of my presence. I startled him but he didn't turn around.

He hung his head. "I'm sorry."

"So am I."

I held him tightly for what seemed ages without speaking. Finally, he leaned over and picked up the box near him wrapped in Christmas paper. "Merry Christmas," he said, handing it to me. "Go on, open it."

He turned to face me as I tore off the paper to reveal a rectangular box the size of a large envelope. Lifting the lid, I discovered it was full of papers.

"Go on, read them," he prompted.

The first sheet was folded. My heart beat fit to burst as I opened it, dreading it was a letter from Billy saying our relationship was over. Phew! It was a bank statement. I could feel tears welling in my eyes, unless it was his way of telling me he wanted half? I blinked. I had to look again. At first I didn't understand. It was impossible.

"What the fuck, Billy?"

There were far too many zeroes. And the mortgage – it had been paid for the next six months.

"Did you do this?" I asked.

Billy nodded. I threw my arms around him, showering him with kisses.

"I couldn't bear to watch you killing yourself. I had to help any way I could."

"Why didn't you tell me?"

"I couldn't. You wouldn't have approved. I saw how you were when you found out. Especially that night you spied on me with Murray and Dale."

"I wasn't spying. I went there for comfort, I was feeling depressed."

"I know. Dale told me afterwards how they'd tricked you. But I knew you were there. I saw your car in the street as I drove up."

I dug him in the ribs. "Watching you was fuckin' hot, Billy."

"Why do you think I stayed for extra time once I knew you were there? Knowing you're watching me make a slut of myself is the ultimate turn on for me."

"And my so-called friends?"

"I soaked them for every penny I could get. Got them to order more expensive pizzas. That's how it worked. The topping was the giveaway. You could order a plain pizza and I'd deliver it and leave. Or you could order from the Pizza with Everything special menu and that indicated what sort of sexual favors were required. I made sure I was the addictive ingredient so some of your friends, like Marty for example, was having pizza three or four times a week. Some of them are still ringing me believing I'm going to leave you."

"I did, too, when you moved into the spare room."

"I didn't like myself very much. I couldn't let you touch me while I was doing that job. I thought if you touched me it would contaminate us, our relationship. I never wanted that to happen. I had to divorce myself from you to get through it."

I felt ashamed. "Shit, Billy. I didn't make it easy for you."

Billy brightened. "You haven't opened all your present."

I dug back into the box and brought out a cardboard folder. I didn't think I could be any more surprised or delighted. I was wrong.

"Holy fuck!" I realized now why Billy had looked so disappointed at the prize-giving. It was because I wasn't there for the culmination of all his hard work when he was awarded the Employee of the Year accolade. "Is this for real?"

"Two business-class tickets to Rome and an all-expenses paid two weeks in Italy at top hotels, plus $5000 spending money."

I remembered Billy in the bedroom. "What did you have to do to win that?"

Billy winced at my accusation. "Just be the best at my job. It wasn't hard. The girls don't like what they do, whereas I love sex. I know how to flatter men. Plus I had no competition from other delivery boys so I got all the gay orders. I won it fair and square."

I wondered for a moment whether I should actually be congratulating my boyfriend for making me a laughing stock, a cuckold, and fucking every horny male with enough money for a pizza special in the neighborhood. Then I thought of all those Italian men and the moment passed.

"Steve, I need to tell you something. Don't hate me for it."

"I know already, Billy."

"What? How?"

"Mario and I snuck into the courtyard and watched."

"You don't think I'm a sick fuck?"

"Why? Because you did it or because you liked it?"

"Both."

"Well, Mario and I must be sick fucks as well, because we both blew the biggest loads you've ever seen while we watched." Billy got a cheeky grin. "You want to do it with your uncle again, don't you?"

He didn't need to answer.

Billy was puzzled. "What are you doing here? What happened to dinner with the family?"

"My family is here." I wrapped my arms around him more tightly.

"She told you about the phone call?"

"Yep."

"What else did she say?"

"That you were a degenerate. But, hell, she wasn't telling me anything I didn't already know."

Billy took that for the joke I meant it to be.

"And, for my sake, please keep on being a degenerate for as long as you live. Merry Christmas, Billy." I took the very personal gift out of my pocket and handed it to him. It was a small black box. Billy flipped the lid open and his eyes lit up just before he burst into tears. While he was sobbing I took out the gold ring that had inscribed on the inside 100% Pure Slut and slipped it on his finger. I handed him the box and he slipped the one engraved 100% Slut Lover on mine.

Then I pushed him roughly down on the rocks, ripped his Speedos off and fucked the ass off him. It had been too long. Much too long.

Lydian Press

About the Author

Barry Lowe writes about love and sex so he won't forget how to do it. When he's not scribbling his adventures for the Sydney gay weekly *SX*, or out doing field research, he's writing about love's wonderful variations for a series of smut eBooks, novels and anthologies for Lydian Press.

Go to www.barrylowe.info

ANTHOLOGIES By Barry Lowe

BUSTING BILLY'S BUTT - eBook & Print

Four On The Floor
Jolly Rogering
The Devil His Due
Never Take Candy from Strangers
Done Like A Dinner
In The Family Way
Right Up His Alley
Group Therapy

THE MAJOR AND THE MINERS - eBook & Print

A Serpent in Paradise
Desperate Remedies
Joshua's Story
Emerald City
Danny's Revenge
Future Tense

ROMANCING THE BONE - eBook and Print

Carbon Dating
Let the Games Begin
Taking the Bait
Party Whip
Team Player
Davy Jones' Locker
Here's to You, Mr Robinson
Gay Dungeon for the Straight Boy
OMG! Santa's Got a Six-Pack
Vlad the Impaler
Meta-Analysis of the Effects of Love on Tofu

LIKE FATHER LIKE SON - eBook and Print

> Man of the Hour
> Like Father Like Son
> Sonny & Shared
> Sonny Side Up
> Eclipse Of The Son
> Son & Games
> Where The Sun Don't Shine
> The Sun Shines Out Of His Ass
> Have Son Will Travel

BEAR SKIN - eBook and Print

> Carbon Dating the Bear
> Bumming a Fag
> Four on the Bear Floor
> Beauty, Mate
> There's a Bear in There
> Busting a Gut
> Steam Punk
> Piss Elegant
> The Bear's Guide to Depilatory Wax

ROUGH & READY - eBook and Print

> Stocks & Shared
> Scarface
> Ceps: Mad about Muscle
> The Plumbers' Mate*
> Climbing Up the Wall
> Little Red Rides da Hood
> The Dex Factor
> Jailhouse Cock
> The Skinhead Upstairs

THE MORE THE MERRIER - eBook and Print

Marine Biology
Flesh for Fantasy
Buck's Night
Four On The Floor
Sluts & Satyrs
Framing the Picture of Dorian Gray
Fuck Buddy
Seven Card Studs
Dude, Where's The Bar?
New Year's Steve

THE BOY IS A BOTTOM - eBook and Print

Marine Biology
Marine Animals
Attack of the Ass Bandits
The Arab Downstairs
Clockwork Derriere
Creaming the Party Dip
Top of the World
Route 666: Signal Driver
The Butler Did Him
Fifty Shades of Fey
Spinning the Bottom

THE GRAVY TRAIN - eBook & Print

In the Soup
Salad Days
Whores d'Oeuvres
Beefed Up and Porked
Torte A Lesson
Café or Lay

BABY, I'M NOT A MONSTER - eBook and Print

The Vampire's Guide to Dental Hygiene
Stupid Cupid
Gadigal
Pride & Joy
Seeing Things
My Dad's a Vampire
Guys & Trolls

COCK-EYED OPTIMISTS - eBook and Print

A Red Rose Before Crying
Too Frocked to Care
The Three Spooges
Love and the Odor of Red Leatherette
It's All Greek to Me
Hard On His Heels
Salted Mixed Sluts
The New Dad's Club

OMG! NOT ANOTHER GAY EROTICA ANTHOLOGY?

OMG! My Dad's a Stripper!
OMG! The College Jock's a Nudist!
OMG! Put Some Clothes On!
OMG! My Uncle's a Fairy!
OMG! Satan Wants a Blow Job!
OMG! My Dad's Got Tits!
OMG! Santa's Got a Six-pack!

For all Barry's titles please visit his page at:
lydianpress.com

Lydian Press is dedicated to bringing you the
finest GLBTQ erotic literature on the web.

Visit us on the web at:
http://lydianpress.com